BERNIE &MAGRUDER
& THE PARACHUTE PERIL

BOOKS BY PHYLLIS REYNOLDS NAYLOR

Phyllis Reynolds Naylor

ALADDIN PAPERBACKS

New York London Toronto Sydney Singapore

First Aladdin Paperbacks edition July 2001
Copyright © 1999 by Phyllis Reynolds Naylor
Originally published in hardcover with the title
Peril in the Bessledorf Parachute Factory

Aladdin Paperbacks
An imprint of Simon & Schuster Children's Publishing Division
1230 Avenue of the Americas
New York, NY 10020

Also available in an Atheneum Books for Young Readers edition.

Designed by Michael Nelson
The text of this book was set in Goudy.
Printed and bound in the United States of America.

10 9 8 7 6 5 4 3

Library of Congress Cataloging-in-Publication Data
Naylor, Phyllis Reynolds.
Peril in the Bessledorf Parachute Factory /
Phyllis Reynolds Naylor.-1st ed.
p. cm.
"A Jean Karl book"
Summary: Bernie's attempt to marry off his sister Delores results in mystery and near-disaster at the Bessledorf Parachute Factory.
ISBN 0-689-82539-0 (hc)
[1. Family life-Fiction. 2. Humorous stories.] I. Title.
PZ7.N24Pe 2000
[Fic]-dc21
98-36606

ISBN 0-689-83166-8 (pbk.)

To the beloved children of
Paige and A. J. Emerson

CONTENTS

BERNIE & MAGRUDER
THE PARACHUTE PERIL

One

THE SIGN ON THE WALL

The Bessledorf Hotel was at 600 Bessledorf Street between the bus depot and the funeral parlor. Officer Feeney said that some folks came into town on one side of the hotel and exited on the other. The Bessledorf had thirty rooms, not counting the apartment where Bernie Magruder's family lived, and Officer Feeney said that if walls could talk, there would be tales of want and woe and unrequited love a'plenty.

Bernie knew what woe was, and he also knew what it was like to want something or need something badly, but he wasn't sure about the love part.

"What does 'unrequited' mean?" he asked.

"Unreturned. Unfulfilled. You love somebody who

doesn't care a fig about you," said Feeney as he ran his nightstick along the rails of a wrought-iron fence, making a ku-*lak*, ku-*lak*, ku-*lak* sound.

"Has it ever happened to you? Unrequited love?" asked Bernie, who certainly hoped it would never happen to him. The only woman he had ever loved was his mom, and for now he'd like to keep it that way.

"Once—long ago," said Feeney. "Her name was Sara Jane. She said she'd always wanted to marry a man in uniform, so I became a policeman, just for her. I'll be danged if she didn't run off and marry a sailor."

"Did it make you angry?" Bernie asked, wishing Feeney would lend him the nightstick so that he could go ku-*lak*, ku-*lak* along the fence.

"Oh, for a while, maybe. But then I decided I'd rather be a policeman than be married to Sara Jane, so I began to feel right thankful to that sailor."

When they got to the corner, Feeney went one way and Bernie the other, back to the hotel where his dad was manager and where his mom wrote romance novels at the registration desk when she had nothing better to do.

Bernie was thinking about his sister, Delores, the oldest of the Magruder offspring. Delores had had plenty of experience with unrequited love, he decided. She'd had so many boyfriends, he couldn't count them all—Steven Carmichael, who married the floozie from Fort Wayne, the great-great-great-great-great-great-grandson of a pirate, even Feeney, for a few brief minutes, anyway. If it was unrequited love you wanted to know about, Delores could probably write the book.

When Bernie walked into the hotel, he stepped over Mixed Blessing, the Great Dane, who was asleep on the mat, he petted the cats, Lewis and Clark, who were perched on opposite ends of the mantel like china figurines, and talked to Salt Water, the parrot, who lived in a cage in the lobby.

"Wanna dance? Wanna dance?" Salt Water squawked, strutting back and forth on his perch. "Awk! Awk!"

"Not particularly," said Bernie. "What's the matter, Salt Water? You lonely?"

Even parrots needed love, Bernie thought, holding a sunflower seed between his thumb and finger and letting the bird waddle over and gently snatch it away.

Bernie ambled around to the registration desk where his mother sat. There were two hundred scribbled pages to Mrs. Magruder's left, a stack of unused paper to her right, and a couple dozen crumpled sheets on the floor.

"What are you working on now?" Bernie asked her. "Did you finish *Quivering Lips*?"

"Why, that was months ago," she told him. "I even

finished *Trembling Toes*. I'm still working on *The Passionate Pocketbook*, about a woman who takes revenge on the man who jilted her."

"Sort of like unrequited love?" asked Bernie.

"Exactly. Only in *this* case, she gets even."

Bernie sighed. Love certainly made the world more complicated.

"Listen, Bernie," said his mother. "Your sister called and said she's been asked to stay after work today for an important meeting at the parachute factory. She needs to look especially nice and wanted you to bring her high-heeled shoes the minute you got home."

"Sure," said Bernie. He liked going to the parachute factory because it was up near the top of Bessledorf Hill, and if he took his skateboard with him, he could coast all the way back down.

He walked down the hall to Delores's bedroom. His twenty-year-old sister had a bed with a pink-and-purple spread on it, a dressing table with a round mirror, a lamp with a fringe around the shade, and about six different pictures of herself on the wall, each with a different boyfriend. In every photograph, the boyfriend had been X'd out with a Magic Marker. The entire hotel was filled with unrequited love, Bernie thought. If the walls could talk, as Officer Feeney said, they'd be singing country love songs from morning to night.

Bernie found the shoes that Delores needed,

stopped in his own room to get his skateboard, then walked up the street and on up the hill to the big white parachute factory near the top.

He sat down in the reception area while the secretary buzzed his sister. The draperies at the windows looked as though they had been made out of parachute silk, tied back in the middle with rip cords. There were pictures on the walls of sky divers floating down from the sky in formation. Of soldiers jumping out of planes. Parachutes over land; parachutes over water. Red parachutes, blue parachutes, yellow, orange, and violet.

Bernie let his eyes travel upward and was surprised to find that a huge white parachute with blue trim was stretched across the entire ceiling, a light fixture dangling from the center.

A door opened from the factory area, and Delores hurried in, looking excited. "Thanks, Bernie," she said, taking her brown pumps with the gold buckles from him. "This could be a really big step for me. A really, really big step. I could get a great promotion, and I've got to look my best at the meeting."

"You're welcome," said Bernie as Delores tucked the shoes under her arm and went back through the door leading to the factory. "Good luck!"

He got up from the green vinyl couch.

"Good-bye," said the secretary.

"Good-bye," said Bernie.

Just before he turned to leave, he saw a sign above the secretary's desk. He had not noticed it before, he'd been so interested in the pictures of parachutes.

It was an important-looking sign printed in bold black letters. There was a black frame around it, and it was protected by glass:

NOTICE TO THE PUBLIC

The Bessledorf Parachute Factory, maker of the world's best-crafted parachutes, unconditionally guarantees that your parachute will open under normal conditions.

We demand the highest workmanship, will accept no inferior products or shoddy substitutes.

To insure that every parachute will open, each of our employees knows that at any time, an inspector may require him to jump from a plane in the parachute he has just completed.

We protect your life as we would our own.

Two

PARACHUTES AND STUFF

Delores was so excited at dinner that evening she had to be reminded to eat. The Magruders sat around the table in their hotel apartment, Theodore, the father, at one end; Alma, the mother, at the other. On one side of the table sat Delores and Joseph, who was a student at the veterinary college. On the other sat Bernie, eleven, and his nine-year-old brother, Lester.

Lester was making a French-fried-potato sandwich, with catsup on one slice of bread and peanut butter on the other.

"My dear," said their father in his dark blue suit to Delores, "it is clear that you will not eat your broccoli until you have related all that happened to you today at the parachute factory, for you are wound as tight as a kite, as high as a clock, and are keeping us all in a state of suspension."

"After our meeting today," said Delores, her eyes shining, "the supervisor put me, *me*, in charge of grommets."

There was a hush around the table.

"So . . . ?" said their mother finally.

"I am Grommet Boss for my workstation, Mother! I, Delores Marlene Magruder, am Grommet Boss for all six employees at my table. Every day I count the grommets, I order more when necessary, and if there's any problem at all, the people at my station come to me—*me*—to make their complaints."

"Wow!" said Lester admiringly. "Do you get a big raise?"

"Not exactly," said Delores. "But I *do* get to keep my coffee mug on a shelf near the supervisor's, instead of on the top of the sink."

"I'm speechless," said Joseph.

"*I'm* hungry," said Bernie. "Do we have any more potatoes, Mom?"

"Delores, my daughter, I am as proud of you as if you had taken over the presidency of the company," said Mr. Magruder. "For just as Rome was not built in a day, and birds must learn to fly step by step and wing by wing, we make our way up in the world, not by leaps and bounds to the applause of the multitudes, but inch by inch along the pebbled shore of frustration and hope."

"What did he say?" Lester asked Bernie.

"He said it might not sound like much, but any success at all for Delores is better than nothing," Bernie whispered back.

"In fact," Theodore continued, "should anything happen to me, God forbid, or to my job as manager of this hotel, you, Delores, are the only other salaried member of this family. It would be you we would look to for support and sustenance, you who would have to provide the food for our mouths and the roof over our heads."

Bernie suddenly wasn't hungry anymore.

"So aim for the top, my dear," Mr. Magruder said. "Reach for the stars. You may become an executive yet, and *that* would provide you with a very comfortable salary indeed."

The Bessledorf Parachute Factory *did* seem to be doing exceptionally well. A story on the front page of the newspaper said that profits were up at the ten-year-old factory, and business was never better. Some of the guests were even talking about it in the hotel lobby that evening. The regulars who lived at the hotel—Felicity Jones, Mrs. Buzzwell, and old Mr.

Lamkin—discussed it as they played cards over by the parrot cage.

"Why, I'd put my life savings in stock at the parachute company if I had any savings," said Mr. Lamkin, placing an ace of hearts on the table.

"If I were a bit younger, I might apply for a job there myself," said Mrs. Buzzwell, in a voice that sounded like gravel going down a tin chute.

"I feel a poem coming on about parachutes," said Felicity Jones, who was a mere wisp of a young woman. Her parents, it was said, who were exceedingly wealthy, paid to have her stay at the Bessledorf for the rest of her natural life, as long as she wouldn't come home too often and recite odes to the moon. Felicity leaned back in her chair, gazed out the window, and began:

> *"Oh, bill'wing cloud of silken white,*
> *That trails the sky in shim'ring light,*
> *Thou doth descend in majesty*
> *To clothe the ground in secrecy.*
>
> *Thy silent path beneath the sun*
> *That heralds when your work is done,*
> *Be gentle to the little folk*
> *Harnessed 'neath your floating cloak . . .*
> *And may you . . ."*

10

"Awk! Awk! Lock the hatch! Lock the hatch!" squawked Salt Water. "Clear the deck!"

"Play, Felicity! Don't sit there jabbering," ordered Mr. Lamkin, and the card game resumed.

When Bernie walked to school the next morning with his two best friends, Georgene and Weasel, he told them about Delores's promotion . . . uh, new position . . . well, *sort* of new position, there at the parachute factory.

"Bernie, did your sister ever finish high school?" asked Georgene.

"Did she ever finish *grade* school?" asked Weasel. "In fact, did she ever make it through third grade?"

"Don't be too hard on her," Bernie said. "Mom says she's doing the best she can with what she's got." But that was the problem. It might not be enough. Bernie had never considered the possibility that Delores might someday have to support them all, and it made him a little sick to his stomach.

The truth was, Delores may not have been a rocket scientist, but she wasn't exactly stupid. A little low in self-esteem, perhaps. This little step up the corporate ladder would do wonders for her morale, and Bernie knew it. He told his friends how he had taken her brown pumps with the gold buckles to the factory the day before so that she might look her best for the conference. And then he remembered the sign on the wall.

"Did you know," he said, "that at any time, a safety inspector can demand that any employee take a parachute he has just completed, strap it on, and jump from a plane?"

Georgene came to a dead stop on the sidewalk and stared at him. "*What?* What if a person's afraid of heights? What if he's afraid of planes?"

"It doesn't make any difference," said Bernie. "He has to do it."

"It's only fair!" said Weasel. "Somebody's life might depend on that parachute. The only way the company can be sure each one is safe is if every employee knows he might have to test it himself."

That made sense. But Bernie, who had never even trusted his sister to make potato salad, was not at all sure he would want her making and folding his parachute.

"Aren't parachutes made on an assembly line, though?" Georgene asked. "Do *all* employees have to jump?"

"Only the person who worked on it last," Bernie explained, "the person who sews the straps and pounds the grommets, and folds the parachute. That's the person responsible for checking it over, to make sure there are no mistakes. That's the person who has to stamp her initials on the parachute, and if it doesn't open, she's the one who gets the blame."

He tried to imagine what would happen if a parachute Delores had checked and stamped failed to open. Would the family of the deceased sue? Would they sue the factory or just Delores? It didn't much matter, he decided, because if they sued the factory, the factory would sue Delores. And if Delores were sued and lost, it would cost the Magruder family all they owned and more besides. Mr. Fairchild, owner of the Bessledorf Hotel, would fire Bernie's father, and soon the family would be out on the street again, blowing about the country like dry leaves in the wind, as his mother was fond of saying. If Father lost his job at the hotel and Delores lost her job at the parachute factory, there would be no money at all.

Bernie had another thought, however—so awful, so selfish, that he tried shaking his head hard to make it go away. But the thought was still there. It was this: If only Delores were sued and not the Magruder family, then perhaps she would just go to prison for a while, the Magruders could stay at the Bessledorf, and Bernie could have her room—the biggest and best bedroom in the whole apartment.

If there was any other way to get a room of his own, of course, he would prefer it. But Delores had had a room to herself ever since the Magruders moved into the hotel. So had Joseph. Bernie and Lester had been sharing a room all this time, and there was nothing Bernie longed for more than a place to call his own. No cracker crumbs left on the floor by Lester, no crazy music bombarding him as soon as he got home from school. No smelly socks and sneakers stinking up the place, no moldy apple cores or pizza crusts to step on underfoot, no disgusting noises waking him at night, no stupid questions, prying eyes, listening ears. No one rummaging though Bernie's things to find a stray nickel or dime.

If Bernie had a room of his own, especially Delores's big room, he could have his friends over to talk in private. Weasel could come to spend the night. They wouldn't have to turn out the light just because Lester wanted to go to sleep. If Delores's room were his, he could fill all her shelves with his baseball card collection and mystery books and soccer trophies and games. Of course he would get rid of her pink-and-purple bedspread and her dresser with the round mirror. But man, he would have himself a room!

At dinner that evening, Delores once again monopolized the conversation, and Bernie suddenly began to wonder if the interest she was taking in her job had anything to do with the fact that she had so often been the victim of unrequited love.

"Delores," he interrupted finally, "would you ever consider giving up your job if you found the man of your dreams and could settle down and raise children?"

"Children just like *her?*" Lester cried in alarm.

Delores haughtily lifted her head. "I hereby

announce that I am through with men forever. I have been jilted, scorned, embarrassed, hurt, rejected, and ridiculed, and I want nothing more to do with men. From now on, I am a career woman, on the fast track within our company. You are looking at a woman on the rise, Bernie, and if I never meet another man on this earth, it will be just fine with me."

Except that at eight o'clock that evening, while Delores was polishing her fingernails behind the registration desk and Bernie had just come in from taking Mixed Blessing for a walk, a stranger came into the lobby—a short, muscular man, slightly balding, with a pleasant square face—and asked for a room.

In the past, a new man checking into the Bessledorf Hotel—*any* man—would have interested Delores. She would have looked deeply into his eyes as she asked his name. She would have inquired politely as to whether there would be a "Missus" registering also and, if he turned out to be single, she would have let her fingers touch his ever so lightly as she handed him his key.

But this time Delores was all business. This time her eyes did not wander, and her voice did not quake.

DWAYNE HOPPER, she wrote in the registration book, and dropped the key in his hand.

Three

DAYDREAMS

"What's with Delores?" Bernie heard Joseph say to their mother that evening as he was preparing to attend one of his night-school classes on Equine Diseases of the Ear. "A new man signed into the hotel and she's not even interested?"

"Now don't badger her," Mrs. Magruder said. "She's got her mind on a career these days. I, for one, wish she would find a husband and settle down, though, because you can't sit in front of the fire in your later years with a bucket of grommets."

"If she does find a husband, I get her bedroom," said Lester, who shared bunk beds with Bernie.

Bernie couldn't believe that Lester had beat him

to it. It just hadn't seemed polite to bring it up before, but Mother didn't even blink, and now Bernie wished he'd put his claim in first.

"I think *I* should have her bedroom. I'm older than Lester," Bernie said quickly.

"We'll see, we'll see," said Mother. "Delores isn't even *thinking* about husbands, so why concern yourselves?"

It was right then, at that moment, that Bernie resolved to do everything he could to interest Delores in Dwayne Hopper and vice versa. If there was a bedroom to be had for the asking, then he was going to do what he could to get it while the thought was on everyone's mind. Should it go to Lester, they would each have a room of their own, of course, but Delores's room was by far the better.

Then he had a second thought. If Delores married and left her job at the parachute factory, it would be only Father again who had a salary. But no matter. If Delores and Dwayne were to marry, they would, of course, buy a house, and then the Magruders could move in with them should anything happen to the hotel business.

"How do you make two people fall in love?" he asked Georgene and Weasel the following day as they sat in the swings on the school playground, turning slowly around and around until the chains were

twisted together in a long coil; then they went spin-
ning in the other direction, letting the toes of their
sneakers scrape the ground, making circles in the dust.

"Love?" chortled Weasel. "Who do you want to fall
in love with you, Bernie?"

"Not me. I want to get Delores married off so I can
have her bedroom," Bernie said, and explained about
the man who had recently signed into the hotel.

Georgene was shocked. "You just picked the first
man to come along so you could have your sister's bedroom?"

Bernie shrugged. "He seemed nice enough. If he's
not right for Delores, she won't fall for him. It's just
that simple."

"I don't think so," said Weasel. "Nothing's simple
about Delores except her brain. I'm glad I've already
got my own bedroom."

"I'm glad I'm an only child," said Georgene.

They were all three quiet for a time, thinking
about the problem, and at last Weasel said, "If you
really want to do it, though—make them fall in love—
I'd write them each a letter and sign the other's name."

Georgene said, "I think animals are the answer.
When a man sees a woman petting a dog, he figures
she'll be kind to their children. And if a woman sees
a man with a cat in his lap, she imagines herself in
his lap, the man stroking her hair, so *she* falls in love.

It's as easy as that. I read it once in a magazine."

Writing love notes and forging their names might be tricky, Bernie thought, but getting each of them together with animals was a cinch.

When the Magruders gathered for dinner that evening, Bernie was surprised to hear Delores announce, somewhat matter-of-factly, that the man who had checked into the hotel the day before, a man by the name of Dwayne Hopper, turned out to be a new employee at the parachute factory. He had, in fact, been assigned to sew straps and pound grommets at the very workstation where Delores was boss.

"Mind you, he's an underling, so don't start looking at us as soul mates or anything," Delores said.

"What's a soul mate?" asked Lester, his mouth full of pork chop.

"A soul mate," said his father, "is that creature of divine disposition with whom your most private thoughts, your most sacred dreams, may ultimately be shared, with whom you pledge allegiance and love until your very breath has ceased to exist within your earthly body."

"What'd he say?" asked Lester, looking around the table.

"He said," said his mother, "that a soul mate is that person with whom you fall madly, passionately, head over heels in love with, as Penelope does in my new novel, which, if it is ever published and becomes a best-seller, shall enable us, dear children, to *buy* this hotel if we so wish, and become its owners instead of its managers."

The family stared in awe, each imagining how their lives might change were they to make the hotel theirs.

"Should that happy day ever come," said Theodore grandly, "I shall name it *Theodore's.*"

"Really?" said Mother, raising her eyebrows. "Indeed! Why not *Alma's,* pray tell? If it were *my* money, Theodore, earned with my own pen . . ."

"You didn't let me finish," Father said hastily. "*Theodore and Alma's,* to be sure. Or even *Alma and Theodore's.*"

"What about the *A and T Hotel,* and be done with it?" Joseph suggested. "If it were *our* hotel, though, we'd allow pets in every room, not just our own pets in the lobby. I could run my own clinic in the basement, and we could provide a pet-sitting business for guests while they were in town."

"I would turn one of the guest rooms into a studio overlooking Bessledorf Street, where I could write my novels," said Mother.

"We could serve anything we wanted in the dining room, too," said Lester. "We wouldn't have to have the kind of food Mr. Fairchild likes, with sauces on the side. We could have jars of peanut butter and jelly on every table."

"*I*," said Delores dreamily, "could buy the kind of clothes that would befit a rising young executive at the parachute factory."

"And I could choose any room I wanted for my own," said Bernie.

Everyone looked at Mother.

"Well," said Theodore, "hadn't you better be getting busy?"

"Yeah," said Lester. "How soon will your book be done? How much do you think you'll make?"

"Let me know if I can be of any help. I could always type it up for you," said Joseph.

"Now don't rush me," said Mother. "I have other duties here, too, you know."

And she did, of course. As soon as dinner in the apartment was over, Mother had to put on her best dress and black stockings and be the hostess in the hotel dining room for the rest of the evening while Joseph took over the registration desk. Father saw to the busboys and waiters, Delores checked the linen supply, Bernie and Lester walked the dog, changed the cats' litter box, cleaned the parrot cage, and generally kept out of their parents' way.

"Guess what?" Bernie said to his friends when they came over the next afternoon to play out in the garden behind the hotel. "We may be going to be rich."

"Yeah?" said Weasel. "I may be going to be president."

"No, really!" said Bernie. They climbed up on the wall by the alley and sat waiting for the chocolate cookies that Mrs. Verona, the cook, was baking in the hotel kitchen. If Mother became rich, they wouldn't have to worry about Father losing his job at the hotel or Delores losing her job at the parachute factory, or waiting until Joseph finished veterinary college and could help with expenses. They would be the family of a rich author and could ride everywhere in limousines.

"How are you going to be rich?" Georgene wanted to know. "Has Joseph discovered a cure for rabies?"

"Mother's going to finish her novel," Bernie replied.

"And?" said Georgene.

"So?" said Weasel.

"So . . . she'll sell it and make a million dollars," said Bernie uncertainly.

Georgene cleared her throat. "What was the name of her first book?"

"*Quivering Lips*," said Bernie.

"Did she sell that one?"

"No," said Bernie.

"What was the name of her second book?"

"*Trembling Toes*," said Bernie.

"Did she sell it?"

"No."

"What's the name of the book she's working on now?" asked Weasel.

"Oh, never mind," said Bernie. He knew as well as his friends that *The Passionate Pocketbook* probably wasn't going to have any better luck.

"Well, anyway, Bernie, we're still friends whether you're rich or not, you know that," said Georgene.

"I know."

"And if you *do* get rich, you know what you should do?" said Weasel.

"What?"

"You should buy the parachute factory. Then you could turn it into this great skateboard factory and build skateboards out of Fiberglas, with colors that light up while you roll, and maybe little parachutes that pop out the back to help you stop. Bessledorf Skateboards would be known all over the world, and at any time an inspector could ask an assembly line worker to go to the top of Bessledorf Hill, get on a skateboard he'd just made, and take it all the way to the bottom, just to make sure it was safe."

Four

THE BIG BLACK HOLE

Theodore was worried.

A phone call from Mr. Fairchild, owner of the Bessledorf Hotel, informed him that something was being built in Plattville, the next town, only ten miles away, and nobody knew what it was.

"Yes, sir?" Bernie's father said, and waited.

Bernie was eating his cereal at the kitchen table when the call came through. He could hear every word, because Mr. Fairchild's voice was so loud that Theodore had to hold the phone away from his ear.

"Sir?" exclaimed Mr. Fairchild, who was calling from Indianapolis. "*Yes, sir?* Is that all you have to say? We've got to find out what it is, Magruder."

"And why is that, sir?"

"Why is that? Why is *that*?" came the voice. "Why, it could be anything at all that they're building, Theodore. And if it's a hotel—a grand hotel with a swimming pool and sauna, with an exercise room and a conference center, with shops selling shoes and shawls and drinking straws—the Bessledorf could be out of business within a year."

Bernie swallowed his bite of cereal, then swallowed again.

"And what is it you want me to do, sir?" asked Theodore.

"Do? *Do*? I want you to find out what they're building. I want to know what it is. You've got to know your competition!"

"I'll do my best, Mr. Fairchild," said Bernie's father.

"Let me know what you discover," the owner said, and hung up.

"What does he think I am?" cried Theodore. "A detective? A private investigator? A spy? A snoop?" And then, to his wife, "I'm too *busy* to go prowling around over in Plattville, Alma! I've got rooms to fill and a banquet to arrange and ceilings to repair . . ."

"I'll go," said Bernie. "I'll get Georgene and Weasel and we'll ride over there on our bikes and find out. It's Saturday. We have time."

"Good for you, Bernie!" said his father. "You are

25

obviously a boy who cannot be held back. A son of infinite curiosity, who will never say no to a challenge. You are destined to be a young man who will scale mountains and cross rivers, who will sail oceans, and—"

"No, Dad," said Bernie, "I'm just going to get on my bike and ride to Plattville."

Weasel had to clean out his dad's garage before he could go, and Georgene had to straighten her room, so when Weasel was done, he rode to Georgene's house, and when Georgene was done, she and Weasel rode together and joined Bernie, who was waiting at the front entrance of the hotel.

Mixed Blessing, of course, wanted to go, too, and ran from window to window on the first floor of the Bessledorf, barking plaintively, but Bernie knew he might get run over, so he left him at home.

"How are we supposed to find out what they're building? Steal the blueprints?" asked Weasel.

"Maybe we could hide in the supply shed and try to overhear what they say," Bernie suggested.

But Georgene just scoffed. "We don't have to steal the blueprints and we don't have to hide in a shed," she said. "We'll just go to the foreman and ask."

The road was flat between Middleburg and Plattville, the air pleasant, not too warm and not too cool. Georgene led the pack, her ponytail flying out

26

behind her, her red sneakers a blur when she pedaled fast. Bernie came next on his green mountain bike, and Weasel brought up the rear, sunglasses clipped over his regular glasses, a baseball cap worn backwards on his head.

They rode past barns and fields and silos and sheds, past creeks and cemeteries, woods and streams, a power plant and a cement factory, until at last they came to the sign that said PLATTVILLE.

Georgene put out her hand to show she was slowing down, and the three of them coasted into the business district, past the school, through the residential area, and at last found themselves on the outskirts of town once again, the highway stretching far out before them.

Bernie yelled to the others and pulled off to the side of the road. All three bikes came to rest by the ditch, all three riders panting.

"We rode all the way through Plattville and didn't see a thing!" said Bernie.

"Maybe Mr. Fairchild made a mistake," said Weasel.

"Mr. Fairchild never makes a mistake. At least, that's what he says," said Bernie ruefully.

"Well, just because it's not on *this* road doesn't mean it's not in Plattville," said Georgene. "Let's go back to the Texaco and ask."

So they turned their bikes around and went back into the business district.

Bernie rode up to a man who was pumping gas.

"We're looking for a building or something that's going up here in Plattville," he said. "Could you tell me where we'd find it?"

"Don't know anything about a building, but there's something going on 'bout a half mile back. Turn left at the first intersection, go 'bout three quarters of a mile, and you'll see it. Don't know what it is, though."

After they retraced their path, turned at the intersection and rode three quarters of a mile, Bernie could see off in the distance a big orange crane, an earth-moving vehicle, a couple of trucks . . .

"There it is! There's where it's happening," he said to the others.

As they rode closer, they could see that all the trucks and machines were standing perfectly still, however. And when they reached the place and got off their bikes, they could see that no one was working on Saturday.

Bernie, Georgene, and Weasel parked their bikes beside a high fence with a sign that said NO TRESPASS-ING and looked at each other. The gate was ajar with just enough space to slip through.

"If they didn't want anyone trespassing, why did they leave the gate open?" asked Weasel. He looked like a spy himself with his dark glasses.

"That's what I was thinking," said Bernie.

"And it's not as though we were going to take any-thing, or bother anyone," said Georgene. "All we want to do is look."

So one by one they squeezed through the gate and walked up the huge mound of earth where tire tracks came in and out. When they reached the other side, they walked fifty feet more until they came to a hole.

It was a deep hole. A dark hole. A large rectangu-lar hole that was half the size of a football field.

"So what is it?" asked Weasel.

"A swimming pool?" Georgene guessed.

"A basketball court? A school?" said Bernie. "How can I go home and tell my dad it's just a hole?"

"Hey!" came a voice behind them, and Bernie jumped so high, he almost slid over the edge.

A security guard was coming up the bank toward them. "Can't you read? It says 'No Trespassing' back there," he yelled.

"We weren't going to bother anything," said Geor-gene. "Nobody's working here, anyway."

"That's not the point," the guard said. "You could get hurt on a construction site. There could be a cave-in or something. Better get on your bikes and go home."

"We just wanted to see what they're building in Plattville," said Bernie.

"So does everyone else," said the guard.

"Then what is it?" asked Georgene.

"Sorry. All I do is guard the place. Can't tell you."

"Why? Is it secret? Are they making bombs or something?" asked Bernie.

The guard laughed. "Even if I knew, I couldn't tell you. The people who are building this want to keep it private. It's their land, their money. I figure they can do what they want with it."

"Well, at some point folks will find out. At some point, everyone will see!" said Georgene.

"I suppose so, when they're good and ready," said the guard. "Now you kids skedaddle before I have to run you off."

It was disappointing, after riding all that way. When Bernie and his friends got back to the hotel, Mrs. Verona had coconut pie waiting for them, and tall glasses of iced tea.

But when Bernie's father came into the hotel dining room and said, "Well?" Bernie had to tell him that all he had seen in Plattville was a deep dark hole.

Five

ANIMAL LOVE

If there were only two ways to get Dwayne and Delores interested in each other, Bernie would choose pets. He wasn't about to compose any love letters unless he had to.

He had to plan this carefully, however. When Dwayne got home, he usually went up to his room until dinnertime. When Delores got home, she helped out at the registration desk or went back to the apartment for a snack.

"Delores," Bernie said on Monday afternoon when she got home and kicked off her shoes. "Mixed Blessing has been missing you."

"Missing *me*? Mixed Blessing doesn't know me from

31

a side chair. The only time that animal even licked my hand was after I'd eaten some fried chicken."

"That's just it. I think he realizes something's missing in his life, and that something is you. He watches you out the window when you leave in the mornings; he waits for you in the afternoons. I think he's shy. He's just not sure how you feel about him."

"So what am *I* supposed to do about it? Tuck him in at night and read him a story?" asked Delores.

"I think if you'd just scratch his ears once in a while or take him for a walk now and then, it might help."

"I'll think about it," Delores said, and opened a bag of potato chips.

At the sound of the crackling bag, Mixed Blessing got to his feet and trotted over to the registration desk. He put his muzzle in Delores's lap, as close as he could get to the potato chips.

"See?" said Bernie. "He must have heard us talking about him."

Delores fed the big mutt some potato chips and scratched his ears. Mixed Blessing wriggled his nose even closer to the bag of chips until his nose was practically in it.

"Okay, boy, I'll take you for a walk in a little while," Delores promised. Bernie just hoped that Dwayne Hopper would be around to see it.

While Delores sat at the registration desk eating

potato chips and feeding them to the dog, Bernie sat over by the window watching for Dwayne. When at last he saw him sauntering up the street with a triple-dip mint chocolate chip cone in his hand, Bernie said, "Delores, I think Mixed Blessing wants to go out right now."

"How do you know? He's not barking. He's not over by the door wagging his tail."

"He's got that look in his eye," said Bernie.

Delores studied the dog's eyes.

"I'll handle the registration desk if you'll take him for a walk. I mean, once you've fed him potato chips and taken him around the block, he's just *got* to know you care about him."

"Okay, okay," said Delores. She slipped on her high heels again, took the leash Bernie handed her, and went out.

Bernie had to smile at the sight of Delores teetering on her high-heeled shoes, trying to keep up with Mixed Blessing, who was far in the lead. Surely Dwayne would see her and admire a woman who loved a dog that much. A Great Dane. How could he not be impressed that the woman who was his boss at the parachute factory could take time from her busy schedule to walk a dog?

Dwayne Hopper was about twenty feet away when he saw Delores and Mixed Blessing coming toward him. He was only ten feet away when the dog saw the triple-dip cone.

"Mixed Blessing!" yelled Delores.

"No!" yelled Dwayne Hopper.

The next thing anybody knew, Dwayne Hopper was flat on his back on the sidewalk, and Mixed Blessing was standing over him, straddling him with his four legs, eating the ice-cream cone.

Uh-oh, thought Bernie as he ran outside.

"You stupid, idiotic dog!" screamed Delores. "You moldy meat loaf! You big bag of baloney. Were you born without a brain?"

Dwayne was trying to get to his feet, and Bernie hoped that Delores would help him up, but she simply grabbed the dog's collar and dragged him back to the lobby of the hotel.

"From now on," she said to Bernie, "he can walk himself. I don't care if he *does* miss me. I don't care if he wants to adopt me. I don't care if I've broken the big galoot's heart. He's all yours." And she bopped Mixed Blessing over the head with a newspaper and went on back to the apartment.

Bernie sighed and waited till Dwayne came through the door.

"I'm really sorry that Mixed Blessing ate your cone," he said. "I'd be glad to get you another. Any flavor you want."

"Oh, it's okay," the man said. "I'm probably getting too fat, anyway."

But Bernie brushed him off and told him that the Magruders would be glad to wash his shirt for him. "Actually," said Bernie, "pets are pretty nice. Mixed Blessing is sort of a handful, but cats are more intelligent. Did you ever have a pet, Mr. Hopper?"

"Well," said the man, "I had a turtle once. Left it out in the garden when we went on vacation, and when we came back, only its shell was there. Don't know what happened to it."

"You can't get very close to a turtle, though," Bernie told him. "A cat, now. Why, if you ever sat down on our couch, I'll bet one of the cats would crawl right in your lap. You give a cat a little attention and he'll think of you as a giant cushion."

"Yeah?" said Dwayne Hopper.

"Try it," said Bernie.

What Dwayne Hopper didn't know, of course, was that Bernie had tucked in his pocket, for just such an occasion as this, a small package of catnip, and as he guided Dwayne to the couch, he tore the package open and slipped it into the man's pocket.

Dwayne Hopper sat warily down on the couch and looked at the cats. Lewis and Clark were up on the mantel, as usual. Lewis was sitting straight up, looking about the room, but Clark was lying on his back, his paws curled over his stomach, tail dangling down over the end.

All at once Lewis began to sniff the air. Next he jumped down off the mantel and began to walk around the room, his nose up, ears alert. About the same moment, Clark's eyes opened wide. His tail came up, his paws went down, and he rolled right off onto the floor and began heading in the direction of the sofa.

Both cats leaped up on the couch, one on either side of Dwayne Hopper. Both began to sniff around, then crawled at once into his lap.

"Well, look at this!" said Dwayne. "Friendliest darn cats I ever saw! Why, they're purring like crazy, Bernie. Just listen to their motors go."

"They like you, that's for sure," said Bernie.

Dwayne began to chuckle as the cats pawed at his thigh. They rolled over on their backs in his lap and sounded like airplanes about to take off.

Bernie went back into the apartment. "Hey, Delores," he called. "Did you ever hear the saying that a cat can tell if a man is honest?"

"No, I never did, Bernie," said his sister, who was reading a magazine and eating an apple.

"Well, come and see who Lewis and Clark are falling for," Bernie told her.

Delores got up and went out into the lobby.

Dwayne Hopper was half-sitting, half-lying on the

sofa with both cats on top of him. One was trying to get into his pocket, the other was licking his shirt, and both acted half crazy.

Delores stood there at the registration desk, hands on her hips. "I don't know about that man," she said. "Anyone who can be knocked over by a dog, or mauled by two pussycats, must not have much between the ears. I want a man with backbone. I want a man with romance!"

"I thought you didn't want any man at all," Bernie told her. "I thought you were going to concentrate on your career."

"You're right," she said. "Thanks for reminding me." And she flounced back into the apartment.

Six

ROMANTIC PERSUASION

Mr. Fairchild was very, very interested in the deep dark hole in Plattville. Every few days he called Bernie's father to ask if anyone had found out yet what the project was going to be.

"All I can tell you, sir," Theodore told him, "is that someone is digging something, but it could be anything from an industrial-size septic tank to an Olympic pool. It is not only a deep dark hole but a deep dark secret, and I must tell you, sir, that I cannot run this hotel and be a private investigator at the same time."

"Very well, Theodore. Understood," said the owner.

What Bernie was interested in was Delores's room. Now that he'd thought about it, the idea seemed bigger and better each time it came again. He could stay up all night if he had his own room. Read! Have his friends over without interruptions from Lester. The more he dreamed about a room of his own, the more he wanted his sister's, and the more he imagined life without Delores, the more he wanted her gone.

If Delores got married and moved out, he promised himself, he'd give her the best present in the whole world. He'd do whatever she wanted at her wedding. He'd even wear a shirt with ruffles down the front and a red bow tie. He'd *dance* if he had to.

That seemed to make it right, somehow, so Bernie set his mind on getting the man in 221 interested in his sister. He and Georgene and Weasel studied Dwayne Hopper every minute that they could. In the evenings, Dwayne Hopper sometimes sat in the big leather chair in the lobby reading a newspaper. He generally ate a late dinner in the dining room, and afterward he might stroll down to the corner to buy toothpaste or a magazine or a bottle of Pepsi.

There was plenty of opportunity for Dwayne to flirt with Delores or Delores to flirt with him, but from all Bernie could tell, they were strictly business.

At dinner one evening, Bernie looked at his sister and said, "How is Dwayne Hopper these days?"

Delores had come to the table in a new blue dress and she held her fork daintily as she lifted some asparagus to her lips. "What do you mean, how is he? Has he been suffering from indigestion or something?"

"What I meant," said Bernie quickly, "is how is he working out at the parachute factory?"

"His work is quite satisfactory," said Delores, pleased that her new position was being taken so seriously. "He learns quickly and is pleasant to be around."

Well, that was encouraging, anyway, Bernie thought.

"Is *pleasant* anywhere close to *passionate?*" he asked Joseph later.

"Hey, Bernie, forget it. Those two aren't going to fall in love," Joseph told him. "You have to have a spark before you can get a flame, you know. As far as Dwayne Hopper and Delores are concerned, they're dead wood."

"But, *why?*" Bernie wanted to know. "She's fallen for every single man who's ever come in the front door except for old Mr. Lamkin."

"There *is* no 'why' where love is concerned," said Joseph. "Wait till she's over her executive kick, and maybe we can marry her off yet."

But Bernie didn't want to wait that long. She might be on her executive kick for another five years. She might be on her executive kick when Bernie went

40

off to college. He'd hardly need a room to himself after that.

"Besides," said Joseph, "I'm not too sure about this man Dwayne."

"How do you mean?" asked Bernie.

"A man who pounds grommets in a parachute factory can't exactly be rich. How can he afford to live in a hotel on a salary like that?"

"He's in one of the cheapest rooms, maybe?" Bernie asked.

"Maybe. But it still seems strange to me," Joseph told him.

It did not seem strange to Bernie, however. So he brought home Georgene and Weasel the next day after school. The three of them locked themselves in Bernie's bedroom—the room he shared with Lester. When they were all sitting cross-legged on the lower bunk, Bernie said, "Okay, I'm going to try your idea. I'm going to send Dwayne a love letter from Delores, and Delores a love letter from Dwayne, and you've got to help me write them. I figure he's not too much older than Delores. They both work at the parachute factory. They both live here at the hotel. . . . How much more alike do they need to be?"

"Lots," said Georgene.

But Bernie refused to be discouraged. "Well, they have to start with something, and parachutes are as good as anything," he said. He tore out sheets from his school notebook and passed them around. "Let's start with the letter from Dwayne to Delores."

"Ugh," said Weasel, running one hand across his face, which was as freckled as a speckled egg. "I never wrote a love letter to a girl in my life."

"Who did you write one to, then? A chicken?" joked Georgene.

Weasel glared at her. "Does it have to be really mushy?" he asked Bernie.

"Just try to pretend you're Dwayne and you want to get Delores's attention. What would you say?" Bernie suggested. And then he settled back against the wall, chewing on his eraser, and stared at the sheet of blank paper.

Weasel rested his head on his hands, elbows on his knees, and frowned down at the notebook paper on the bedcovers. Georgene leaned against the windowsill and looked thoughtfully through the glass, tapping her pencil against her cheek.

The room was very, very quiet.

Suddenly a soft *crunch, crunch, crunch* came from somewhere.

"What was *that?*" asked Weasel.

"I don't know," said Bernie. "Listen."

The three sat so still, they could only hear soft noises inside their heads. They listened some more, but all was quiet.

"How long should this letter be?" asked Georgene.

"It's got to be short. The more we say, the bigger the chance we'll blow it. Just look at it as your one chance to persuade Delores that Dwayne is in love with her, and vice versa."

The three friends settled down again and thought some more. Georgene scribbled a line or two on her piece of paper, then scratched it out.

Crunch, crunch, crunch. The noise came again.

Georgene and Weasel and Bernie looked at each other. Bernie put one finger to his lips. The noise seemed to be coming from under the bed.

Slowly, slowly, Bernie leaned over until his head was hanging off the edge. He looked underneath.

Lester was lying on the floor beneath the bunk beds, holding a giant bag of potato chips.

"What are you *doing?*" Bernie asked.

"Eating," said Lester.

"Why are you under the bed?"

"Because I wanted to hear what you guys were talking about. When I heard you coming, I hid."

"You were listening! You were spying!" Georgene cried.

"Yep!" said Lester, sliding out on his belly. He scooted over to one corner, propped the bag of chips between his knees, and continued eating.

"So what did you hear?" Bernie demanded.

"I heard that you're going to write love letters to

Delores and Dwayne and make them think they're in love."

Bernie's shoulders slumped. "Lester, if you *tell* . . ."

"What'll you give me not to?"

"That's blackmail!" said Georgene. "That's illegal."

"So is writing letters and pretending they're from somebody else," said Lester.

Bernie sighed. "Okay, so what do you want to keep quiet?"

"A half-pound Hershey's bar, milk chocolate, no nuts," said Lester.

"Okay. Get out and don't tell anybody, now or ever, what we're doing," said Bernie.

For the next fifteen minutes the three friends suggested and scribbled and read aloud their romantic phrases, for the votes or vetoes of the others. A letter from Dwayne to Delores was especially difficult for Bernie because he could not think of a single reason any man in his right mind would want to fall in love with his sister.

At last they decided on the two letters:

Dear Delores:
    I have not been able to tell you before how my heart beats faster when you come into a room, when I hear the sound of your voice or

smell your perfume. Is there any hope that we could ever be more than friends?

Let me be the man in your life when the stress of your demanding job is over for the day.

With admiration,
Dwayne Hopper

Dear Dwayne:

This may come as a surprise to you, but I think we have a lot in common. Parachutes are not my whole life. Do you want to have dinner sometime and talk it over?

Fondly,
Delores

"Good!" said Bernie. "Georgene, you copy the letter to Dwayne, and Weasel, you copy the letter to Delores. If I write the letters, Delores might recognize my handwriting."

The letters were carefully copied onto plain white writing paper. Then Bernie slipped one in the mail cubicle of room 221, and the other, folded into a neat little square with Delores's name on it, he left on the registration desk for her to find when she came home.

Seven

A LITTLE HELP FROM FELICITY

They seated themselves on the couch in the lobby where they had a full view of the registration desk. All Bernie wanted was to be able to see Dwayne's and Delores's faces when they read the love letters.

"What if Delores reads the letter we left for her and slaps Dwayne in the face?" asked Georgene.

"Then I guess we can rule out a wedding," said Bernie, "and I'll be sharing a bedroom with Lester for the rest of my life."

They pretended they were watching old Mr. Lamkin's favorite soap opera, *No Tomorrow*, in which beautiful Lily Malone had been jilted by the young heart specialist, Dr. Blake. Dr. Blake had just made his

46

last rounds of patients for the night and was getting ready to leave the hospital, when he was called to the bedside of a drowning victim, and it turned out to be Lily Malone, who had thrown herself into the river because her heart was broken.

Mr. Lamkin was crying quietly into the big red handkerchief he kept stuck in his back pocket.

At that moment the glass doors to the lobby swung open, and Dwayne Hopper came in, stepping over Mixed Blessing there on the mat and stopping at the news rack to buy a paper. Finally, after scanning the front page, he walked up to the desk and asked Mrs. Magruder if there was any mail for 221.

"I don't believe there is, Mr. Hopper," Mother said, pausing from the writing of *The Passionate Pocketbook* and looking around at the mail cubicles behind her. "Oh, I beg your pardon, there is," she said, and handed him the folded piece of paper, the letter Georgene had carefully copied.

"Thank you," said Dwayne Hopper. He walked toward the elevator, unfolding the paper as he went, and began to read. Suddenly he stopped dead still, blinked, and seemed to be reading the letter again. Bernie saw him swallow. He nudged Georgene on one side of him, Weasel on the other. The man moved swiftly toward the elevator, pressed the button and, when the doors opened, stepped in.

47

"Well, at least he read it," Weasel said.

"He sure didn't wait around for Delores to get home, though," said Georgene.

As if on cue, the lobby doors swung open once again, and in came Delores, her high heels clicking as she stepped over the dog and clacked across the marble floor.

"Ah!" said Mrs. Magruder. "I'm glad you're here. I want to go have a cup of tea before I study tonight's menu. How did your day go?"

"About the same. I have to admit, Mother, that I love being Grommet Boss. I think I was born for management. I absolutely adore telling other people what to do," Delores said.

"I'm sure you're very good at it," her mother said. "Incidentally, here's a letter for you. I found it on the desk this afternoon."

Mother gathered up her manuscript and pen and headed for a little table in the hotel restaurant, where she ordered a cup of tea.

With their faces turned toward the television but their eyes turned toward Delores, Bernie and his friends watched and listened.

"What . . . ?" said Delores so suddenly that Mr. Lamkin looked over from his chair in the corner, Mrs. Buzzwell stopped playing solitaire, and Felicity Jones, who was smelling a rose over by the window, turned to stare.

Slowly Delores raised one hand to her face and reread the letter. *"What?"* she said again, but more softly. And then she covered her mouth and kept reading.

"Time to go," Bernie whispered. "I don't want to be around if she gets suspicious."

The three went outdoors and sat on the wall next to the alley.

"I sure hope this works. I really want her room," said Bernie.

"It's not as big a deal as you might think," said Georgene. "I have a room, and Mom's always after me to keep it straight."

"Yeah," said Weasel. "I'm not in my room half the time, anyway. Mostly I'm over here."

"That's my point," said Bernie. "We need a private place where we can talk."

At dinner that evening, Delores was more quiet than usual, but she didn't say a single word about Dwayne Hopper.

"How are things working out at the parachute factory?" asked Mr. Magruder from his end of the table. "How is our Grommet Boss today, my dear? How many heads have you turned and how many hearts have you broken?"

Delores blushed just a little, and for a moment Bernie thought she was going to tell the family about the love letter with Dwayne Hopper's name attached. But she suddenly turned very businesslike again and said, "I am a young executive on her way up the corporate ladder, Dad. I haven't time for romance."

Bernie's shoulders slumped. Lester kicked him under the table, but Bernie kicked back.

"Surely, my dear, there is room for both in your life," said Mother. "Look at me! I'm a mother, I'm manager of the hotel dining room, and I'm even an author on the side."

"Except that you've never had anything published, Mother," Joseph said gently. "I don't believe that a person is entitled to be called an author until she actually has something in print."

"A writer, then," Mother corrected. "But, someday, Joseph, you will see my name and photograph above a rack in the bookstores. I will be dressed in flowing chiffon, my hair done up in ringlets, my gown slipping delicately off one smooth white shoulder, my bodice slightly unlaced, and my . . ."

"That's enough, Alma," said Theodore quickly. "Let us not exhibit lust in front of the children, for lust and dust doth corrupt what thieves break in and steal."

"Huh?" said Lester.

"He said not to get mushy in front of the kids," Bernie answered.

What Bernie couldn't figure out was why Delores didn't say anything about the love letter. In the past,

Bernie's sister was more than happy to tell the family about every man who fell in love with her—more than they cared to know, in fact. According to Delores, half the men in Middleburg had been her boyfriend at one time or another, even though they didn't deserve her. Was it possible she didn't believe the note? Could she suspect that Bernie and his friends were behind it? No, Bernie decided, if Delores thought he had written the letter, she would have got right up from her chair, walked around the table, and stuffed the paper in his mouth.

The only thing Bernie could figure was that the writing wasn't good enough. Maybe he needed to follow it up with a second letter, better written. The obvious person to ask, of course, was his mother, since she wrote romance novels and would know exactly what a woman wanted to hear. But that was out of the question, so Bernie turned to the only other woman he knew who might possibly be able to help: Felicity Jones.

He went out in the lobby after dinner, but Felicity wasn't there. So he put the leash on Mixed Blessing and took the Great Dane for a long walk around Middleburg Park, where the dog sniffed every lamppost, marked every bush, chased a few pigeons, and went splashing through the fountain. By the time Bernie got him home again, Felicity Jones had finished her evening meal and was now sitting in one corner

51

of the lobby, looking out the window at the moon.

Bernie went over and sat across from her. "Excuse me," he said. You always had to begin slow with Felicity, because the slightest thing could startle her. "Felicity, could I ask a big favor?"

Felicity's eyes finally detached themselves from the moon and settled on Bernie.

"I know you write poems," Bernie said. "Really good poems. And I wondered—if I paid you a dollar—could you write a poem for me?"

"Why, certainly, Bernie, but poetry is priceless, you know. I couldn't possibly accept any money."

So much the better.

"Well, then, I would really appreciate it if you would write a poem to give to someone, only you've got to keep it secret."

"All right," Felicity agreed, smiling.

"It's supposed to be kind of a . . . no, I mean, it *is* a love poem to a girl that a person doesn't know very well yet, but wishes he did."

"I see," said Felicity. "Without naming any names, Bernie, could you tell me about this person so I could make the poem more personal?"

"Uh, no! It's just got to be a general sort of poem."

"All right," said Felicity. "I'll sit in this corner, and the moon can help me write it. Come back in an hour and pick it up."

Bernie sat on the wall outside the kitchen door, swinging his legs and watching the moon. Funny how two people could be watching the moon at the same time, one of them writing poetry and the other one trying to see if he could lift the lid off a garbage can with his feet. When he went back inside later, Felicity was done and handed him a sheet of paper on which she had scrawled:

O lady fair,
Whose lustrous lips
From love's sweet bloom
The honey sips,
I bid you favor
With your smile
This humble slave
You do beguile.

For if you turn
A stony stare
Upon my face,
I should not dare
To ask of thee
The greatest bliss,
To be rewarded
With your kiss.

Eight

MORTIFICATION

Bernie wanted to show the poem to Georgene and Weasel the next day before school, but he accidentally left the house without it and had to go back. By the time he ran up the steps of Middleburg Elementary, the last bell had rung and he slid into his seat like a runner reaching first base.

Now he'd have to wait until recess to show the poem to Georgene and Weasel, so the three could decide whether or not to sign Dwayne Hopper's name to it and give it to Delores. But when Miss Raleigh began the study of latitude and longitude, Bernie's head began to nod and he looked across the room to see Georgene staring dreamily out the window and Weasel with his eyes half closed.

So when the teacher had her back to the class, drawing horizontal lines on a globe she had sketched on the blackboard, Bernie reached across the aisle, poked Weasel in the arm, and handed him the folded piece of paper.

Weasel sat up, pulled his glasses up onto the bridge of his nose, and read the poem. His eyes opened wide.

"Shakespeare?" he whispered.

"No. Felicity," Bernie whispered back. "Should I give it to Delores and sign Dwayne's name?"

"She'll never suspect *you* wrote it, for sure," Weasel said.

Miss Raleigh looked around. "Do I hear whispering?" she asked.

Bernie and Weasel sat like stone, so the teacher turned back again and began drawing vertical lines this time.

"Pssst! Georgene!" Bernie whispered, looking in the other direction.

Georgene glanced over.

Bernie leaned way over, across the empty seat on the other side of him, until he could reach Georgene's outstretched hand. At that very moment the teacher turned around.

"All right," she said. "Which way is that note going?"

Georgene and Bernie froze, like two statues with

their fingers touching, Michelangelo's *The Creation of Adam* or something.

"Bernie, is that a note from you?" asked the teacher.

Bernie swallowed. "Yes, ma'am."

"Will you bring it to the front of the room, please?"

Bernie felt all the blood in his body rush to his face. He took the note back from Georgene and slowly got to his feet. He went to the front of the room and handed it to the teacher, but she wouldn't take it.

"No, I don't want your note," she said. "Is this class a public or a private place?"

"P-public," said Bernie.

"Then I assume that everything said in this class is open to the public. Would you please face the class and read the note aloud so that we can all share it?"

Bernie thought his legs would collapse beneath him. He stared out at the grinning faces, all but Georgene's and Weasel's.

"Well," said the teacher. "We're waiting."

"It's : . . it's private," said Bernie.

"So you were carrying on personal business in a public place," said the teacher.

"Yes, ma'am."

"You may have your choice. You may either read the note to the entire class, or you may take detention for the rest of the week—one hour after school each day."

Bernie was about to take detention when he realized that if he did, he would miss Delores coming home from the parachute factory and Dwayne as well. Now that the flame had been kindled, he had to be there to keep it going.

He swallowed again. "I'll read it," he said, and began:

> "'O lady fair,
> Whose lustrous lips
> From love's sweet bloom
> The honey sips, . . .'"

The class began to giggle.

> "'I bid you favor
> With your smile
> This humble slave
> You do beguile.
>
> For if you turn
> A stony stare
> Upon my face,
> I should not dare
> To ask of thee
> The greatest bliss,
> To be rewarded
> With your kiss.'"

The class broke into howls of laughter, and Bernie's face was as red as the stripes on the flag. He hastily took his seat as Georgene sat with her eyes on her desk and Weasel buried his head in his arms.

"Thank you, Bernie," said Miss Raleigh, very much surprised at the poem. "I'm sure Georgene appreciates your sentiments, but next time, tell them to her outside."

The kids were still teasing Bernie and Georgene at recess.

"You dork!" Georgene said to him. "How could you do that, Bernie? I was mortified! I've never been so embarrassed in my life!"

"How did I know Miss Raleigh was going to turn around right at that moment?" Bernie said. "What do you think? Should I give it to Delores or not? Will she believe that Dwayne wrote it?"

"Even if she *does*, what happens after they fall in love and start to compare notes?" asked Weasel.

Bernie hadn't thought of that. He lay down on the grass and stared up at the leaves on a tree above. "Okay, here's the deal," he said finally. "If they *do* fall in love, and Delores confesses it was his letters that won her over, do you think Dwayne is going to tell her he didn't write them? And the same with Delores?"

"Probably not," said Georgene. "And even if they

do admit it, if they really *are* in love, it won't matter."

"Yeah, that's the way I see it," said Bernie.

But Weasel wasn't so sure. "Just be sure that the poem Felicity wrote doesn't get published somewhere under Dwayne Hopper's name." he cautioned.

Life sure is complicated, Bernie thought on his way home from school that day. It would be easier to *build* another room onto the Magruders' apartment than to make Delores and Dwayne fall in love. And even if they did, how could he be sure they would marry? And even if they married, was that any guarantee that Delores would move out? What if Dwayne just moved *in* instead? That would mean seven people using one bathroom!

Nevertheless, Weasel signed Dwayne Hopper's name to the poem, and when Bernie got home from school, he placed it on the registration desk once again. And once again, when Delores found it, her cheeks turned pink and she slipped the poem in her pocket without a word.

After dinner that night, Bernie helped Joseph trim Salt Water's claws. Joseph wrapped a towel around the bird so it couldn't flap its wings, and Bernie held the beak so it couldn't peck. Joseph did it as fast as he could, but it still wasn't one of the parrot's favorite things to have done.

"I think maybe Delores really *is* falling in love with

Dwayne Hopper," Bernie said, trying to get a reaction from his brother.

"Well, I hope she finds out a little more about him than she knows now," said Joseph.

"Why? You still think it's strange that he lives here?" asked Bernie.

"I think it's strange that he gets on a bus and leaves town every weekend," said Joseph. "I've been noticing that about him. Not that there's anything wrong with leaving town, but I'd hate to think he's leading a double life, that's all."

"Awk! Awk! Double trouble!" cried Salt Water.

There was only one way to find out, Bernie decided. He wanted Delores to marry and leave home, but he didn't want to see her hurt. He would invite Georgene and Weasel to go with him, and the next time Dwayne Hopper went to the bus depot, they'd follow.

So the next Saturday, all three were waiting in the lobby when Dwayne Hopper came down to breakfast. They watched him finish his coffee and boiled egg in the hotel dining room. When he went outside, they went out, too. When he walked next door and into the bus depot, they entered the depot—at a comfortable distance. And after he left the ticket counter, Bernie went up to the man at the window and said, "We're with him," nodding toward Dwayne Hopper, who was heading toward a far corner of the waiting room. "We need three tickets."

"Oh. Going to Plattville, huh?" the clerk said, and started to ring up the tickets.

"Uh . . . how much is it?" asked Bernie.

The clerk totaled up the price of three tickets.

"Oops, sorry! I guess we don't have enough money," Bernie said, and with the ticket man staring after them, the three friends left the depot and went outside.

"Plattville," Bernie said. "What do you suppose he finds so interesting there?"

"A girlfriend?" suggested Georgene.

"An old army buddy?" said Weasel. "A bowling alley? A movie theater?"

"Plattville doesn't have a movie theater or a bowl- ing alley, either one," said Bernie. "I don't know about girlfriends."

They were quiet for a moment, and then Georgene said, "You've got to tell Joseph, Bernie. If there's some- thing fishy about Dwayne Hopper, we'd better find out before we write any more love letters."

Nine

FRAZZLED

If Delores wasn't in love, then she was falling apart, Bernie decided.

She didn't come to the table at night and complain as she usually did. In fact, she didn't say much at all. She came to meals in her high-heeled shoes and earrings, kept her feet crossed at the ankles, chewed with her mouth closed, and excused herself when she sneezed. If Bernie hadn't known better, he would have thought she belonged in another family.

On the other hand, her mind seemed to have gone to live somewhere else, because Bernie frequently found her buttering her sausage instead of her toast, putting a second sweater on over the first, washing her breakfast dishes twice, and trying to write with the wrong end of a pencil.

On this particular night when Delores asked for the catsup, then dreamily poured it into her tea, even her father noticed. "Delores, my girl," he said, "either your mind is addled, your brain is scrambled, or birds are nesting inside your head. What on earth is wrong with you these days?"

"Why, what do you mean?" said Delores, stirring her tea with her fork.

"You simply aren't yourself, my dear," her mother told her. "If I didn't know better, I'd say you were in love."

And suddenly, to everyone's amazement, Delores leaned back in her chair, covered her face with her hands, and broke into tears. "I am!" she sobbed. "Wonderfully, deliriously, hopelessly, unalterably in love."

"Oh, man!" said Lester. "I hope that never happens to me. Is she going to throw up, Bernie?"

"Maybe," Bernie told him.

"Then it is cause for celebration, my dear, not tears!" said Theodore. "Love is the balm that soothes life's cares, your respite in a time of stress. It droppeth as the gentle rain from heaven upon the earth beneath, and helps the corn to grow."

"Huh?" said Lester. "Love can do all that?"

"Oh, it *is* wonderful! But now that I'm an executive, Dad, I'm not supposed to fall in love with under-lings," Delores said.

"Are underlings the same as underwear?" asked Lester.

"No," Bernie told him. "They're the people she bosses around at work."

Delores began weeping again. "It's a passion that can never be enjoyed, a longing that can never be ful-filled, a craving that can never be indulged, and I am perfectly miserable."

"An unrequited love!" said Bernie.

"That's not true!" said Delores. "He loves me just as much as I love him. Oh, he writes the most *won-derful* letters!"

Lester kicked Bernie under the table once again.

"Really?" said Mother. "Well, where there's a will there's a way. Who is the man, Delores?"

"Dwayne Hopper," said Delores. "But no one must know, or it might affect my executive status."

"Dwayne Hopper?" cried Mother. "The man here in our hotel?"

"Well, congratulations," Joseph said to Delores. "By announcing it at this table, you might as well have put up a billboard. It will be all over the hotel by tomorrow."

"This is a family, and that is a family secret," said Theodore, looking sternly around the table. "I expect everyone to respect Delores's privacy, and tell no one—*no one*—what Delores has confided in us. When a sister reveals her soul, it is to be protected as a tender bud. If Delores's love is to flourish and grow, we must never forget that the slightest rumor can break its stem, halt its march, pinch its flower, and plunge Delores into the abyss of despair."

"Wow!" said Lester.

"My dear," said Mother, looking at her daughter. "When did all this happen? You never said a word! You never let on!"

"I was trying to keep it secret," Delores said, drying her eyes on a corner of the tablecloth. "When Dwayne first checked in, I was determined to ignore him and concentrate on my career, but he has won my heart. He may work in a parachute factory, but underneath he has the soul of a poet."

"He writes poetry, too?" gasped Mother.

Delores put one hand over her heart and cast her eyes to the ceiling:

> "'*O lady fair,*
> *Whose lustrous lips*
> *From love's sweet bloom*
> *The honey sips, . . .'*"

"My goodness!" said Mother. "To think we have a real poet staying in this hotel!"

"But what lady is he talking about?" asked Lester. "What lips?"

"My lips," said Delores. "He *loves* me, Mother. Oh, it's a terrible choice I have to make! Dwayne or my job. A husband and family or an illustrious climb up the corporate ladder. Which shall it be? Love or fame and fortune?"

"Exactly how far up the corporate ladder would you be able to climb, Delores?" asked Joseph dryly, taking a bite of peas. "Two rungs? Three? Four?"

"Well, I'm only on the first step, but if I can make Grommet Boss, why not supervisor? And if supervisor, why not manager? If manager, why not a vice president, and if vice president, why not commander-in-chief?"

"Will we go to live in the White House?" asked Lester.

"Delores, my girl, you are indeed a woman of ambition, but let's not be too hasty here," said Theodore. "Let's not take the bull by the horns and forget that he bucks. Let's not swing by our heels without a net and throw the baby out with the bath. First things first. What do you know about this man, and has he actually proposed marriage?"

"Not exactly," Delores answered. "But a man doesn't go around telling just *any* girl that she has lustrous lips, does he?" She looked quickly around the table. "Well? *Does* he?" she demanded.

"*I* certainly don't," said her father.

"Besides," said Delores, looking demurely down at her napkin. "We sometimes play footsie under the worktable at the factory. I slip off my shoes, and Dwayne slips off his, and he caresses my pinkie with his big toe, and . . ."

"Gross!" said Lester.

"So here I am, caught between two loves!" Delores wailed. "If I give up Dwayne, I will be without a husband, but if I give up my career, I will never know the thrill of power, the smell of the greasepaint and the roar of the crowd."

Mrs. Magruder reached across the table and took Delores's hand. "My dear, let me give you some advice. Take whatever comes first. If you are really offered a vice presidency at the parachute factory, take it, by all means, even if it means you cannot marry an underling. But if Dwayne proposes first, marry him."

"Sound advice! I agree!" said Theodore. "A bird in hand is worth two in the bush, and a chicken in every pot is better than a goose on the run. But he is a rather strange duck, isn't he—living here in a hotel?"

"Just tell me this," put in Bernie. "If you *do* marry Dwayne Hopper, you'll move somewhere else, won't you?"

"Of course," said Delores. "And I don't think he's strange at all, Dad. He says he has a home in the country."

"Then what's he doing in Middleburg?" asked Joseph.

"Working his way up the corporate ladder, like everyone else. I just happen to be a little higher than he is, that's all," Delores answered.

Theodore, however, looked perturbed. "Joseph has a point," he said. "If Dwayne has a house in the country, why is he living in a hotel? And if he has money to live in a hotel and own a home besides, where does it come from? Surely not from his salary at the parachute factory."

"He says he wants to learn the business starting at the bottom," Delores explained.

"Well, then, that is admirable indeed," said her father. "Delores, my dear, I wish you the best, and your secret is safe in the bosom of the family. No one must know your affair of the heart. Is that clear, Bernie? Lester? Joseph?"

"Yes," said Bernie and Lester together. Joseph nodded.

For the next few days, Bernie studied Dwayne Hopper every chance he got. Not once did he see Dwayne and Delores rush into each other's arms or sit out in the garden kissing. But whenever they passed in the doorway, they blushed. They whispered sweet nothings over the registration desk and let their hands touch ever so lightly when Dwayne picked up his mail. When Dwayne was around, Delores was twice as frazzled, three times as clumsy, and four times as forgetful.

If this isn't love, thought Bernie, *what is?*

But Joseph remained troubled. "I don't think Delores knows any more about Dwayne Hopper than she knows about horse farming," he said. "When Dwayne gets on a bus this Saturday, I'm going to follow and see where he goes."

"To Plattville," said Bernie.

"Yes, but what does he do there? Who does he see? We've got to find out before she makes any rash decisions."

When Saturday came, Dwayne Hopper ate his breakfast as usual. Then he went next door to the depot, as usual, bought a ticket as usual, and got on the bus to Plattville. Just before the doors closed, Joseph got on the bus, too, wearing a pair of dark glasses, and soon the bus left the station.

When Joseph returned three hours later, Bernie, Georgene, and Weasel were waiting for him at the depot.

"Did you follow him?" asked Bernie.

"Yes, at a distance. I don't think he ever knew I was there," said Joseph.

"Does he have a girlfriend?" asked Georgene.

"Not that I know of."

"Did he see anyone at all?" asked Weasel.

"He met a man at the bus station, and they walked off together."

"What did they *do?*" asked Bernie.

"It's hard to say, exactly," Joseph said thoughtfully. "They went over to this big construction site and stared down at a deep dark hole. Something's being built, but I couldn't find out what. The walls are starting to go up, but that's all I could see."

"Maybe it's Dwayne's house in the country! Maybe he's building it for Delores! Maybe he's rich!" said Bernie eagerly.

"Maybe," said Joseph, but he continued frowning as he went on down the street toward the Bessledorf Hotel.

Ten

BAD NEWS

"Well," Bernie told Georgene and Weasel, "it worked. Delores fell for Dwayne's love letters, and I guess he fell for hers, because they've been playing footsie under the worktable at the factory and whispering together in the lobby. All we can do now is wait."

The three friends had each bought a death-by-chocolate cone at the Casablanca, and they sat on the steps of the library feeling rather proud of themselves.

"Of course," Georgene added, "if they really *do* marry, Bernie, there's still a lot of stuff you have to put up with before you're rid of Delores."

"Like what?" asked Bernie. As long as he had chocolate ice cream in his mouth, he felt he could take anything.

"Like a wedding."

"So what? It'll be Delores getting married, not me."

"But you'd be a member of the wedding party, Bernie. You'd have duties."

"What kind of duties?"

Georgene looked at him thoughtfully. "You're too old to be ring bearer, so you'd probably be an usher."

"So?" said Bernie.

"So you'd have to wear a tuxedo no matter how hot the day was, and a bow tie that practically chokes you. You'd have to go to the rehearsal and remember where to seat the bride's family and the groom's family. You'd go to the rehearsal dinner and eat chicken with some kind of sauce on it, and you'd have to meet all of Dwayne's relatives and remember their names, and who wasn't speaking to whom, and how not to sit them together. On the day of the wedding you'd have to be ready for all sorts of emergencies, like the bride throwing up at the altar and stuff, and then at the wedding banquet you'd have to dance with everyone's grandmother and, worst of all, kiss Delores good-bye."

Bernie began to wonder if it would be worth having a room of his own after all. The thought of having Delores throw up at the altar possibly, and having to dance with grandmothers was almost more than he could take, but for a room of his own, maybe he could do even that.

When the three had nothing else to do, they talked about their favorite subject—how to get their names in the *Guinness Book of World Records*. They had hoped for a while that they might win the record for the longest coast downhill on a skateboard, but as it turned out, Bessledorf Hill wasn't all that steep, and Bessledorf Street wasn't all that long, so that even if they did manage to coast all the way through the business district, they would still come to a dead end in a cornfield.

They had each considered trying to blow the world's largest bubble of gum, until one exploded in Georgene's face and hair, and her mother told her she could never chew bubble gum again. They also were trying for the world record in holding their breath under water, but Weasel said Houdini had already done that, so they were stumped.

"Maybe we could see who could sleep the longest. We could all go to bed when we get home from school some Friday and see if we could sleep till it's time to go back on Monday," Weasel suggested.

"It's probably been done," Georgene told him. "What about seeing who could eat the most peanuts?"

"We'd get sick and barf," said Bernie. "And the peanuts you barf don't count."

It was on Friday afternoon when Bernie was changing the newspapers on the bottom of Salt

Water's cage that a scream like a fire siren filled the lobby. Mixed Blessing rose up on his haunches and immediately proceeded to howl, the cats made a dash behind the couch, and Salt Water, squawking, "Call the police! Call the police!" flew madly around the ceiling, making Mrs. Buzzwell, Felicity Jones, and old Mr. Lamkin duck for cover.

Bernie turned to see where the awful noise was coming from. It was coming from Delores, who had just managed to get inside the door of the lobby before she let loose with her wail once again.

"Delores, pull yourself together!" ordered her mother. "You'll scare the regulars."

Salt Water was already leaving droppings on the floor.

Mrs. Magruder rose from her seat at the registration desk and hustled her distraught daughter back to the Magruders' apartment. Lester had come running out, sure that there was a fire downtown, and Theodore had lurched out of the hotel dining room, armed with a skillet to fend off the attack of whatever wild beast was threatening the guests.

Everyone converged in the Magruders' kitchen where Joseph was making himself a cheese sandwich.

"What is it? The end of the world?" Joseph asked.

Delores plunked herself down in a chair, her mouth as wide as a cave. "The e-end of my fabulous career!" she sobbed. "I've fallen down the ladder, and I'll n-never climb up it again."

"What happened?" asked her father.

"I got demoted. I'm back to lowest woman on the totem pole again, and it's so humiliating!" Delores wept.

"But *why*, my dear?" cried her mother. "What happened?"

"The supervisor said I've been making too many mistakes. I have pounded on grommets upside down, I have sewn on straps every which way. Oh, Mother, I *know* that love and a career don't mix, for I have been distracted by love, and now I will never be an executive."

"Never mind that," said Bernie, anxiously. "Will you marry Dwayne? Will you still move out?"

"I'll have to marry now," Delores wailed again. "It's all that's left for me."

"But has he *asked* you?" the whole family chorused together.

"Not exactly, but maybe now he will. Because the good news is that our love does not have to remain a secret. I am no longer his boss. We are simply two love-struck coworkers, and when two coworkers marry, the Bessledorf Parachute Factory gives them a twenty-pound turkey to begin their married life."

"Wow!" said Lester.

"Well, dear, maybe it's all for the best. I hope

Dwayne's home in the country is not too far from here, so that after you're a married woman, we can see you from time to time," said her father.

"It's in Plattville, I think," said Delores.

Bernie and Joseph looked at each other. So that *was* what was going on in Plattville! Dwayne Hopper was building a country home for him and Delores to live in!

Bernie followed Joseph outside later when they let the cats out for the night.

"I guess Delores will have a house with a whole lot of bedrooms in it," Bernie said.

"If that's what he's building, and he's really in love," answered Joseph.

"I don't think he'd be building a house for her unless he *was* in love," said Bernie.

"I guess not," said Joseph, though he didn't sound very sure about it. "But he was building it even before they got chummy, remember."

When Bernie and his friends went to Middleburg Park on Saturday to ride their bikes along the river, Bernie talked about the fantastic house Dwayne Hopper was building for Delores.

"That hole was big enough for a bowling alley!" Bernie said. "I'll bet that house is going to have a swimming pool, too."

"And probably a movie theater," said Georgene. "Maybe he's a millionaire who goes around the country seeing how the simple folk live. When you go to visit them after they're married, Bernie, will you invite us?"

"Sure! I'll ask if we can have my twelfth birthday party there. I'll invite everyone from school!"

"If Delores marries a millionaire, you'll get so snooty you won't want to hang around with us anymore, maybe," said Weasel.

"Yeah. Delores will probably pay to send you to a private school where they wear blue jackets and red ties and start each day with the school song," said Georgene.

"No way will I ever forget you!" said Bernie. "Think of all the stuff we've gone through together."

"Remember the ghost?" said Georgene. "The blue ghost of the boy who used to live in the hotel?"

"And the bodies that kept appearing and disappearing?" said Weasel.

"And the Mad Gasser? The Mad Bomber? The pirates?" said Bernie. "I wouldn't have had half the fun I've had if you guys weren't around. Besides, the only private school Delores would ever send me to is a military academy where you have to get up at five in the morning and polish your boots."

Delores seemed all gentleness, however, when Bernie happened to walk through the garden behind the hotel that evening. His sister and Dwayne Hopper were sitting in the swing there in the roses, and Dwayne was declaring his love.

"My dear, my darling," he was saying, grasping her

hand. "How could you think I wouldn't love you just because you're no longer my boss? Now we can sit together in the lunchroom, we can hold hands on the walk home. We can gaze into each other's eyes at the drinking fountain, and take an evening stroll through Middleburg like ordinary sweethearts."

"Truly?" said Delores, still sniffling. "Will you be just as proud of me now that I'm back at my old job, simply sewing straps and pounding grommets? When it's not me looking over your shoulder, telling you that you're not doing it right?"

"On the contrary, I shall love you more when you are sitting across the table from me, not criticizing me at all. Now we are equals, and had I known when I took a job in this factory that I would meet the woman of my dreams, I would have come much sooner, so as not to lose a minute of life with you."

Oh, brother! thought Bernie. This man wants every minute possible with Delores? Bernie would gladly give him some of his own minutes if he could.

He shrank back into the bushes and from there, sneaked back into the hotel. What on earth did Dwayne Hopper see in Delores, and why would he be building a magnificent house for *her?* In fact, if he was rich enough to build a magnificent house, why was he sewing straps and pounding grommets in a parachute factory? To learn the business from the bottom up, as Delores said? It didn't quite make sense.

Eleven

FROM BAD TO WORSE

On Monday after school, Weasel went to his trumpet lesson, Georgene went to the dentist, and Bernie walked Mixed Blessing, keeping Officer Feeney company as the policeman made his daily rounds.

The officer poked his head in the doorways of jewelry stores and shoe shops, saying good morning to the two little ladies who ran the bakery, ordering a coffee-to-go at the Sweet Shoppe.

Mixed Blessing, of course, had to sniff every bush, every lamppost, every fire hydrant. And every cat within a city block ran the other way and hid when it saw the Great Dane coming down the sidewalk, almost as tall, from the tips of its ears to its front paws, as Bernie himself.

"So what's happening at your place these days, Bernie?" the officer said, sipping his coffee as they moseyed along. "I hear by the grapevine that your sister's in love."

"Who's been talking?" asked Bernie.

"Well, seems that Mrs. Buzzwell overheard a family conversation coming from your apartment and told Felicity, Felicity told Mr. Lamkin, and now everyone wants to know when the wedding will be."

"Dwayne has to ask her first," Bernie said. "But we heard that he's building a big country house in Plattville. If they marry, I guess they'll live there. And I, of course, will get her old bedroom."

"Plattville, huh? Didn't hear of any houses being built over that way."

"Oh, yes! In fact, Georgene and Weasel and I rode over on our bikes and saw! It's going to be big, all right."

"Well, that's good, then," Officer Feeney said. "Delores deserves a little happiness in her life, and as long as it's not me who has to marry her, I wish her the best."

At the corner, Feeney went on across the intersection to check out the stores on the other side while Bernie went once around the courthouse, then took Mixed Blessing home.

When he walked in the hotel, however, he

thought he had made a mistake and walked in the funeral parlor instead, for the place was as quiet as a morgue.

Mother sat at the registration desk, her eyes as large and round as coat buttons. Father stood stiffly behind her, hands on her shoulders, as though posing for a portrait, Lester was standing like a statue beside his father, Joseph was leaning against the wall, his arms folded, and Felicity Jones, Mrs. Buzzwell, and old Mr. Lamkin sat side by side on the couch staring at Delores, who had sunk down in a chair, her feet out in front of her, arms dangling over the sides, looking as though she had just been run over by a steamroller.

"What happened *now?*" asked Bernie, since nobody else seemed to be saying a thing.

"Delores is gonna die," breathed Lester.

Theodore promptly rapped his youngest son on the head with his knuckles.

"She will do no such thing!" he declared. "Delores is a Magruder. A *Magruder!* And Magruders are trustworthy, loyal, dependable, considerate, generous . . ."

"So what is she going to do? Join the Scouts?" asked Bernie impatiently, trying to make sense of the situation.

"Jump from an airplane," said Lester.

"What?" cried Bernie.

"It seems," said his father, "that the safety inspector paid a surprise visit to the parachute factory today, and he thinks that our delightful, dutiful daughter Delores assembled her parachute wrong."

"He had me so rattled, Dad! So frazzled and discombobulated!" Delores wailed. "He was walking about the factory in his starched white coat, asking all these questions and staring at us through his thick glasses. I'll admit, I may have pounded in some grommets upside down in my time, and sewn a few straps on backwards, but I have never, ever, folded a parachute wrong so that it wouldn't open. I make it a point, when I get down to the nitty-gritty, to do important things right."

"Then you have nothing to worry about, my dear, but fear itself."

"But I was so *nervous*, I couldn't think! He just kept staring and staring. And all this in front of my former underlings, too. It was so embarrassing! Now it's all over town!"

"Then don't jump," said Mother. "Just tell the man he drove you to distraction, and you shall not make the jump."

"It's either that or be fired," said Delores. "We had to sign a contract when we were hired that if ever we were asked to jump out of a plane in a parachute we had completed, we would agree to do it or forfeit our jobs."

"Wow!" said Lester. "She could be splattered all over Middleburg!"

"Will you shut up?" Theodore bellowed, rapping Lester on the head again. "This is your sister we are talking about. Your *sister!*"

"Where's the parachute now?" asked Joseph.

"The inspector confiscated it. I won't see it again until just before I get on the plane."

"When are you scheduled to do it?"

"Friday at eleven o'clock in the morning. It's like an execution," Delores said, and began to weep.

"Delores, if there is any chance you did not put that parachute together properly, you must forfeit your job before you forfeit your life," her mother said.

"I've *got* to do it!" Delores wailed. "If I don't, it will be like admitting that I do shoddy work. I'm not a Grommet Boss anymore, Mother, and if I don't make the jump, I'll be unemployed. A nothing! Dwayne Hopper will never ask me to marry him then."

"She has nothing to worry about," Theodore said confidently. "Our girl is a Magruder, and Magruders have honor. She does not shirk her work. She does not shrink from the task at hand. When a test of courage is called for, a Magruder accepts it gladly. Magruders welcome challenge, thrive on change, seek out the difficult, go where angels fear to tread, feed a fever and starve a cold."

Joseph cleared his throat.

"Delores, what does Dwayne Hopper say about all this? What does *he* think you ought to do?"

"Yes," said Theodore. "What does your future husband say?"

"He . . . s-says he has one hundred percent confidence in me, and knows I'll do just fine."

"He *wants* you to jump?" Bernie asked.

"Like a fish out of water?" asked Mrs. Buzzwell from the couch.

"Like a cat from a car?" asked Felicity.

"Like a bug from a box?" asked old Mr. Lamkin.

Delores slowly got to her feet. She straightened her jacket, lifted her shoulders, and took a deep breath. "I'm going to do it," she said.

"But you still have us, darling," said Mother, dabbing at her eyes with a tissue. "You don't have to jump. So what if you're fired? You can live here in the bosom of your family, and could earn your livelihood scrubbing toilets and floors. You wouldn't starve."

"No, Mother," said Delores resolutely. "I will show the safety inspector how wrong he was about me. I will show the world I have guts."

"Yeah, especially if they're splattered all over Bessledorf Street," said Lester.

"That's *enough!*" Theodore bellowed, rapping Lester on the head for the third time. "At least once in every life, my boy, a person is called upon to stand up and be counted, and this time it's your sister's turn. Where is this jump to take place, Delores?"

"Middleburg Park," Delores answered.

"We shall be there," said her father. "Your family is one hundred percent behind you, my girl, and I daresay that when your beloved sees you so sorely tried and tested, his heart will beat with admiration, his eyes will glow, his pulse will soar, his lungs inflate, his flesh crawl, and his ankles swell. In fact, my dear, I am hereby asking Joseph to gather his combo together for the occasion, and as soon as we see the parachute open, billowing against the clouds, they shall play 'The Wild Blue Yonder,' and you shall float down to earth like the angel you are, on gossamer wings, in a trail of gratitude and glory."

"Whatever," said Delores, and went off to change her shoes.

Twelve

PROFILES IN COURAGE

At dinner in the Magruder apartment that evening, everyone came to the table as sober as though it were the last meal they would ever have with their sister. Lester even handed her the catsup bottle first.

Delores herself didn't have much appetite, Bernie could tell, and he wondered how he would feel if his sister really were to die. Would getting her old room seem so important to him then?

"Dad," said Bernie, "if every person gets the chance to stand up and be counted, what did you do with your chance?"

"Bernie, I'm glad you asked that," said Theodore grandly, unfolding his napkin and spreading it over his lap. "There was a time—a long time ago before you were born—before I met your mother, even—when I was a used-car salesman. We were expected to sell a certain number of cars each week, and as it happened, a week came along when I was short of my quota. In fact, with Saturday approaching, I still hadn't sold many at all."

Theodore helped himself to the applesauce and looked around the table where his four children were watching him.

"What did you do, Dad?" asked Joseph.

"Well, a man came in, sort of down on his luck— I could see he didn't have much money—and after looking over a few cars, it seemed to me he was about to settle on an old sedan that I knew for a fact had a lot of problems under the hood. My boss was offering a bonus to any salesman who could get rid of it."

Theodore took a bite of pork chop and chewed thoughtfully. "I knew that if this poor man bought that car, it was only the start of his problems. He'd never have the money to fix what was wrong with it, so I told him the car wasn't worth his time or money, and sold him another instead."

"What did your boss say?" asked Bernie.

"He was angry, all right. Said we had a fish just ready to bite, and I'd let him get away. Said that old sedan had been sitting on our lot for the past six months, and he didn't want it sitting there for six more, and what kind of salesman was I, anyway, to talk a customer out of a car?"

"Wow!" said Lester.

"Did he fire you, Dad?" asked Joseph.

"Well, no. To show my boss I was a man of integrity who would not cheat a customer to make his quota, I . . . uh . . . bought the Buick myself."

"Buick?" said Mother. "That awful green thing you were driving when we married? That horrible, hideous car that broke down seven times on our honeymoon?"

"Better us than that poor man who was down on his luck, my dove," said Theodore.

"What did *you* do when *you* had to stand up and be counted, Mom?" asked Bernie. "What was your moment of courage?"

"I married your father," said Mrs. Magruder.

"Well, I had a moment of courage," said Joseph. "It was last year when I had to enter an abandoned house and rescue some cats and a litter of kittens. We suspected that one of those cats was rabid, but we didn't know which one. Nobody else wanted to go in there and face those animals, so I put on my protective clothing and in I went. Turned out that none of them was rabid, just wild. Feral cats, hadn't an ounce of civilizing about them. I came out with my gear shredded in a million pieces, but those cats are all adopted now, and all but one is housebroken."

"You make a father proud, Joseph. You're a Magruder through and through," Theodore told him. "Bernie, I hope you can live up to your brother's moment of courage."

"I already have!" said Bernie. "Remember the Bessledorf ghost, and how I stayed up all night to see it and finally figured out what it wanted in our hotel?"

"I'd almost forgotten," said Theodore. "Why, this family has courage to spare, and then some! Lester?"

Lester, however, couldn't think of anything courageous he had done to equal that of the rest of the family, and neither could Delores.

"That's why I'm going to jump on Friday," she explained. "Then you will all be proud of me, and Dwayne will be honored to have me for his wife."

Lester seemed perturbed, and when the family scattered later to perform their evening duties, he said to Bernie, "I'm going to take a long rope, climb to the top of the church steeple, and lower myself down to the ground."

Bernie stared. "Why?"

"So I'll have my moment of courage."

"That's not courage, Lester; that's stupidity," Bernie told him. "Courage is when you do something noble or dangerous because it has to be done—somebody's life depends on it or something. You don't just do it to see if you can."

"So mountain climbing is stupid?"

"Well, not exactly." Bernie was confused. "But if you fall and break your neck, nobody will say how brave you were. They'll say, 'Too bad about Lester; what a dweeb.'"

"There's got to be something I can do! I don't want to be the only one in the family who hasn't stood up to be counted!" Lester complained.

"Try cleaning out our closet; dig out all the dirty socks from under our bunk beds. *That'll* be a real test of courage," Bernie told him.

The news of Delores's coming jump was all over the hotel in an hour, all over town by the following day. In fact, when Bernie came to breakfast the next morning, his father was staring at the banner headline:

LOCAL WOMAN TO JUMP FROM PLANE

"Wow, Delores! You're famous already, and you haven't even jumped!" Bernie told her.

"What does it say, Dad?" Delores asked.

"If you will all sit down, I will read it aloud," said their father, beaming at his daughter. "I *knew* the Magruders would make their mark here in Middleburg!"

"Yeah," muttered Lester, "just splat in front of the library, I'll bet."

Theodore pushed his eggs aside and adjusted his glasses. Then he began to read:

"'Delores Magruder, age 21, an employee of the Bessledorf Parachute Factory, will jump from a plane Friday morning to prove that the parachute challenged by a safety inspector had been properly constructed.

"'Factory regulations specify that every employee must be prepared to use in a test a parachute he has completed if challenged by an inspector. Failure to do so means automatic dismissal and loss of benefits.

"'Miss Magruder was challenged yesterday by O. C. Myers, from the State Board of Safety Inspectors, who purportedly noticed some irregularities in her work. The jump will take place on Friday morning at Middleburg Park.'"

Delores was clearly delighted to see her name in the paper, and fretted that they hadn't included a photo of her also. She was only halfway through her toast, however, when there was a commotion in the lobby. As soon as Theodore opened the apartment door, a horde of reporters and cameramen crowded into the family kitchen and began snapping pictures of Delores, who perched on the edge of the table, legs crossed, chin tilted upward, running one hand through her curly blond hair.

"Are you quite confident the jump will be successful?" called one of the reporters, scribbling on his notepad.

"I am," Delores answered. "I intend to fully indicate myself."

"*Vindicate*," Joseph corrected her.

"Are you at all frightened?" asked another.

"Absolutely not. I have full confidence in my ability to put a parachute together properly."

"And for the spectators, Ms. Magruder, what shall we be looking for as you descend?"

"I will be wearing a pink Spandex jumpsuit with white kidskin boots," Delores answered.

"The parachute, I mean," said the reporter. "What color is the parachute, providing, of course, that it opens?"

"It is a billowy cloud of white with a blue border," Delores told him. And then, to a photographer who was edging toward the refrigerator to get a closer shot, she instructed, "Please take all photos from the left, gentlemen, if you please. That's my best profile. Thank you."

Thirteen

PARACHUTE FEVER

"Theodore, I'm afraid this is all rather going to Delores's head," Mrs. Magruder said after the photographers and reporters had gone, and Bernie and Lester were getting ready for school. "I'm afraid she'll enjoy it so much, she'll want to try it again."

"Nonsense," said her husband. "She's a Magruder through and through, and Magruders don't go in for cheap thrills. We do not trade our reputations for commerce, sell out to promoters, nor cast our bread upon the waters lest it grow soggy and sink to the bottom."

The phone rang, and Bernie answered. But as soon as he heard the voice at the other end, he handed the phone to his father. "For you," he said.

Once again, Mr. Fairchild's voice could be heard

across the entire kitchen: "Theodore, it's all over the newspapers here about your daughter. You are a genius, sir! People will be coming from far and wide to see the jump, and I want my hotel to be ready. I have ordered three hundred swizzle sticks with little paper parachutes on top, to be rushed to the Bessledorf. I want one served with every drink. I want a banner on the front of the hotel, reading, 'Home of Delores Magruder, Test Jumper.' I want a whole new menu planned for Friday, specialty dishes with names like Pilot's Pilaf, Soft-Landing Potatoes, Artichokes à la Airplane, and Parachute Pudding. And your dog—what's its name?"

"Mixed Blessing," said Theodore.

"I want that Great Dane fitted up with a leather pilot's cap and goggles and a flight scarf around its neck. Same for the cats and that parrot, if you can manage."

"Yes, sir," said Theodore.

Mother rolled her eyes.

"And, Theodore, give your daughter my best wishes. If she makes it, you get a raise."

When Father hung up, Mother said, "About pandering to commerce, you were saying?"

"Never mind, my dear, there is work to be done. I'll get Wilbur Wilkins to string up the banner, and you tend to Friday's menu," said Theodore, looking around for the hotel's handyman.

"And if the parachute doesn't open, Theodore? If our daughter is killed?"

"We cannot cast a shadow on her courage, Alma. We cannot dilute her fortitude with fear, sully her resolutions with indecision, muddy her resolve, rain on her parade . . ."

"Oh, stuff it!" Mother cried impatiently, and Bernie and Lester stared, for they had never heard her talk quite like that to their father.

Georgene and Weasel were waiting for Bernie out on the sidewalk.

"Is Delores really going to do it?" Georgene asked.

"I guess so," Bernie said.

"Hey, Bernie, one way or another, you'll get her room!" Weasel joked.

"It's not funny, Weasel! I didn't want to get her bedroom this way," Bernie said angrily.

"If I know Delores, though, she wouldn't put herself in danger," Georgene said, trying to reassure him. "She's always been good about sticking up for number one, and I don't think she'd have agreed to do this if she wasn't one hundred percent sure about that parachute."

"Unless she's more afraid of losing Dwayne Hopper. She says he's all she's got to live for, now that she's fallen off the corporate ladder," Bernie told them.

When they got to school, Bernie was immediately

besieged by his friends, who gathered around to ask questions.

"What if the parachute doesn't open, Bernie?"

"Is your mom going to watch?"

"Has Delores really been putting parachutes together wrong?"

"If it doesn't open but she lives, will she go to jail?"

"She's really going to jump," Bernie told his friends. "I don't know any more than that."

Miss Raleigh announced that the class would make a field trip to Middleburg Park on Friday in order to see the historic jump. Bernie began to feel sick. Especially when his teacher handed out the new spelling word list: rip cord, parachute, insurance, liability, notoriety, precarious, and mortality.

In science that afternoon, they had to study the principles of aerodynamics, in history they read a book about the Wright brothers, the librarian showed a filmstrip on Amelia Earhart, and they finished up with an account of the paratroopers in World War II.

"Man, Bernie, this town is going crazy!" Georgene said as the three friends walked home together. "What will they think up next?"

They were soon to find out. They went up the driveway of the funeral parlor as they sometimes did to see who might be lying in the drive-in window. Whenever the three of them came together, they triggered the electric eye, which mistook them for a car full of relatives, come to pay their respects. Instantly soft music would begin to play, a light would come on in the drive-in window, the curtains would part, and whoever was most recently deceased could be seen laid out properly in a coffin in the window. If there was no body to respect, then the newest in streamlined coffins would be on display.

This time, however, Bernie gasped. Georgene and Weasel frankly stared. For there in the window was a white coffin with a little pink-and-gold angel dangling from a small white parachute suspended over it. A card read JUST IN CASE . . .

And as if that weren't enough, when Bernie, Georgene, and Weasel walked in the front door of the hotel under the huge banner about Delores, they found Mixed Blessing wearing a leather pilot's helmet, flight goggles, and a huge silk scarf, which kept tripping him as he went skidding about the lobby.

Lewis and Clark, the cats, would have none of the nonsense, of course. Two tiny pilots' scarves lay in tatters on the floor, and only the cats' tails were visible from behind the couch. A little parachute was suspended over the top of Salt Water's cage, however, and he hopped rapidly from one end of his perch to the other, chirping, "Jump, girl! Pull the chord! Eeek! Squawk!"

The lobby itself was filled with people, all wanting to get a room early so as to be sure to be in Middleburg the day Delores jumped. They had binoculars around their necks, field glasses in their pockets, cameras in their hands, and were talking excitedly about the best place to observe the jump and whether or not the event would take place if it rained.

When Delores came home from work that day, everyone in the lobby clapped and cheered, and Bernie noticed that she was wearing her best dress, her silver high-heeled shoes, and lipstick so red and bright, it looked as though someone had pasted a rose on her mouth.

She flounced through the lobby stopping to pose for photographs, holding babies and hugging children, while their awestruck parents snapped pictures.

"You're so brave," said the women.

"Good luck, Delores," said the men.

"I'll always remember this," little girls told her.

"We'll be watching Friday!" said the boys.

But just before Delores opened the door to the Magruders' apartment, a twelve-year-old boy ran out from the crowd and yelled, "Miss Magruder, just one more, please?" Delores turned to flash him a big smile, and after the boy took the picture, he called to his mother, "Hey, Mom! We could get 'before' and 'after' pictures. This could be the 'before' picture. Then, *splat!*, the 'after.'"

Delores wasn't smiling when Bernie followed her back into the apartment.

"Joseph," she said to her brother, who was drinking a Coke in the living room. "Do you think most of the people out there are coming to see me jump or to see me kill myself?"

"Both," said Joseph. "They're coming to see the jump, of course, but if you manage to kill yourself, they don't want to miss it."

"That's awful!" cried Delores.

"That's human nature," said Joseph. "Maybe you ought to change your mind."

"Never," Delores told him.

Delores was quiet that evening, and Mother tried to perk her up.

"My dear," she said, "why don't we invite your boyfriend for dinner tomorrow? We haven't had a chance to talk with him much, and I think it would be nice if we got to know him a bit better, especially if marriage is on his mind."

"Good idea," said Delores. "Dwayne is going up in the plane with me, you know. I don't think I could do it if he weren't by my side."

"Is he going to jump with you?" asked Bernie.

"No, but he'll hold my hand till I make the leap," Delores said.

Bernie didn't know why, but every time he thought of Dwayne Hopper going up in the plane with Delores, he imagined him holding her hand till she got to the door, and then—pushing her out into the great beyond.

Fourteen

THE MAN WHO CAME TO DINNER

Middleburg was going nuts.

The news of Delores's impending jump had made the wire services and had appeared in so many newspapers that there were no more rooms at the hotel.

Campers pulled into town waiting to set up tents in Middleburg Park; Officer Feeney had to work overtime just to direct traffic. The chamber of commerce had hung little parachutes from every lamppost, and people lined up at the Bessledorf Hotel just to take pictures of Mixed Blessing in his pilot's cap and goggles.

At dinner on Wednesday evening, the table was set in the Bessledorf apartment with Mother's best china and silver. There was a goblet at every plate, and rose-colored candles in the holders.

"Lester," Delores threatened as she tied a lacy apron around her waist. "Don't even think of talking with your mouth full. Don't even dream of spilling your milk, picking your teeth, gargling your water, licking your fingers, or making any disgusting noises whatsoever. Do you understand?"

"Am I breathing too loudly for you?" Lester asked plaintively.

"I want Dwayne to think we are civilized. I want him to know we can be as genteel as the next person. I want him to be able to picture himself in the bosom of our family. I want to have at least one meal here in the Magruder apartment that does not embarrass, horrify, shock, or humiliate me. Is that perfectly clear?"

Lester nodded.

Dwayne Hopper arrived at a quarter of six carrying a box of long-stemmed roses, which he presented to Mother, having carefully taken out the most beautiful rose of all, which he gave to Delores after kissing her hand.

"Let's vomit," Lester whispered to Bernie, but Bernie poked him hard and Lester faced forward again.

"This is so kind of you," said Dwayne. "Even though the food here in the Bessledorf Hotel is delicious, a man does long for a home-cooked meal with congenial friends."

"Any friend of Delores's is a friend of ours," said Theodore, shaking his hand. "Birds of a feather flock together, you know, and never foul their nests . . ."

"Dad!" said Delores sternly.

"Meet my wife," said Theodore, turning to Bernie's mother.

Mrs. Magruder, still holding the roses, clasped Dwayne's hand. "You have been so kind to our daughter," she said, "that the least we can do is invite you to dinner. It is a time like this that a girl needs a friend, someone she can rely on, who will see her through good times and bad, thick and thin, for richer or poorer, in sickness and health, till . . ."

"Mother!" said Delores.

"Well, I must see to the soup," Mother said quickly. "We are just about ready to begin, so Dwayne, if you will sit here between Joseph and Delores. . . . Bernie and Lester, across the table from them, please. . . ."

Mother brought in the soup, cream of asparagus, and they all took their seats, Father at one end of the table, Mother at the other. The meal began.

"I understand you've been working at the parachute factory for a month now," Joseph said to Dwayne Hopper as he passed the crackers. "What line of work were you in before?"

"Oh, I've always been interested in things that move in the wind," Dwayne said. "Things that flap and wave and catch the breeze. I like a product I can make with my own two hands, from start to finish, bow to stern."

"I have heard that you are in the construction business, too," said Father. "That is, I have heard that you may have something under construction out in the country."

"Well, yes, in a manner of speaking," Dwayne said pleasantly, smiling around the table. "It isn't quite mine yet. What I mean is, it will eventually belong to others, too. . . ."

Delores cast her eyes demurely down at her plate and blushed.

"Actually, we've been keeping it somewhat secret until the time is right," Dwayne said. He picked up his water goblet and took a long drink.

Slurrrrp, came a noise from across the table.

Everyone stopped eating and stared at Lester, who suddenly froze with a huge mouthful of soup, then swallowed, choked, and immediately buried his face in his napkin.

"As you were saying . . . ," Mother said sweetly, turning to Dwayne again, but by this time Dwayne was concentrating on his salad and then the bread, saying what a nice flavor fresh rosemary gave to a loaf of home-baked bread. Bernie realized that he had lost his chance to find out if the country house Dwayne was building had a swimming pool or not.

"Tell me, sir," said Theodore, "do you feel that this is a good area to settle down in? You seem a man of the world, and I imagine you have traveled a lot."

"Oh, yes, I've seen many a country besides our U.S. of A.," said Dwayne, "but let me tell you, there is no place like home. I have seen the east, I have seen the west, I have been north, and I have been south, but when I settle it will be here in Indiana, the heartland of America."

"Indeed it is!" said Theodore, beaming. "I myself have never regretted bringing my family to Middleburg. For some years before that, we were blown around the country . . ."

". . . like dry leaves in the wind," chorused the family, they had heard it so often.

"But now," Father continued, "I find Middleburg to be an ideal location for instilling family values in one's children. Middleburg, Plattville, any of the surrounding towns, of course. . . ."

"Of course," said Dwayne.

Delores collected the soup bowls, her fingers touching Dwayne's ever so lightly, Bernie noticed. Then Mother brought in the veal roast and the garlic potatoes, and the baked apple slices with ginger.

"Tell me," said Dwayne, cutting his meat with enthusiasm, "do you two women share equally the culinary talent, or does mother teach daughter, or daughter the mother?"

"Oh, Delores is every bit as good a cook as I am!"

Mother said hastily, neglecting to tell Dwayne Hopper that the food they were eating at dinner had been cooked by Mrs. Verona, the chef in the hotel dining room.

"Well, I don't believe I have ever tasted a better meal in my life," said Dwayne.

"Wait'll you see dessert!" said Lester. "Big fat gobs of ice cream with massive chunks of chocolate brownies in it smothered by a ton of caramel sauce and . . ." He was actually drooling out one corner of his mouth, and Bernie had to kick him sideways under the table.

Bernie studied the man across from him and tried to figure out what he was thinking. He certainly *seemed* nice enough—not like the great-great-great-great-great-great-grandson of a pirate that Delores had fallen for once, or Steven Carmichael, who had jilted her, or any of the other men who had come into Delores's life briefly and left in a hurry.

"Are you really going to go up in the plane with my sister?" he asked.

"I am indeed," said Dwayne. "I will hold her hand until the very end—until she jumps, I mean. And I am confident that she will land safely amid the cheers of her fellow townspeople."

"How can you be so sure?" Bernie persisted.

"Because a woman as lovely as your sister would not—*could* not—make a parachute that would be a danger to anyone. That she is willing to show the world the faith I have in her—that she has in herself—makes me admire her all the more."

Mrs. Magruder's eyes brimmed over with happy tears. "Oh, Dwayne," she said. "It is such a pleasure to meet a man of integrity, who thinks as much of our daughter as we do. Please consider our hotel your home for as long as you want to stay, until the two of you . . . that is, until the home you are . . . until . . . uh . . . well, as long as you want to stay."

"Thank you so much," Dwayne said, and gazed deeply into Delores's eyes.

What have I done? Bernie wondered. Was it the love letter he had written for each of them that had started it all? Would he be sorry he had brought them together, or was it all for the best? How would he know?

When Dwayne had gone that evening and Delores was talking excitedly to her parents in the kitchen, Bernie followed Joseph to his room.

"Well, what do you think?" he asked.

"I think that Dwayne Hopper is a real smoothie," Joseph said. "Did you notice that not once did he say the word 'love'? Not once did he say the word 'marriage'? He didn't even say he was building a home for *Delores*—only that it would belong to others as well as to himself. Delores just assumed he meant her and

106

their children. Mom and Dad and Delores are reading into things just what they want to hear."

"But if he's *not* in love with her, and he *doesn't* want to marry her or move her into his new house, what's he doing here?" Bernie asked.

"That's what I intend to find out," said Joseph. "And maybe you can help, Bernie."

Fifteen

LESTER TRIES AGAIN

By Thursday morning, the day before the Big Jump, Middleburg was like a carnival. There were tents all over the park, campers lined up along Bessledorf Street, venders selling paper parachutes with Delores's picture on the front.

Wilbur Wilkins was on the roof of the hotel with a megaphone, telling motorists not to block the hotel entrance. Hildegarde, the red-haired cleaning woman, was standing under the canopy with a mop, ready to whack anyone who took the space. Cars were even pulling into the funeral parlor driveway to park, setting off the music-and-light show, and when the curtains opened in the drive-in window, the culprits

108

were horrified to see a coffin containing a sign that now read PARK OUT THERE AND YOU'LL BE IN HERE. They left in a hurry.

At breakfast, Delores looked somewhat pale, Bernie thought, and he noticed that her hand trembled slightly as she drank her coffee.

"You okay, Delores?" he asked.

"Of course," she replied. "I am going to prove myself so courageous that Dwayne Hopper cannot rest until he has asked me to be his wife."

Bernie knew that, difficult as Delores was to live with sometimes, he would still miss her should anything happen. Miss the familiarity of her grumpy face at the breakfast table, if nothing else, and the shrill rasp of her voice at dinner. Her hair curlers in the bathroom sink, and her undies drying from the towel rack.

Georgene and Weasel were waiting for him at the corner.

"How did the dinner go with Delores's boyfriend last night?" Georgene asked.

"Okay, I guess. He seems nice enough," said Bernie.

"Nice enough for her to give her *life* for?" Weasel asked.

"We don't know that that's going to happen," Bernie said.

"No, but it could."

"Why don't we ride over to Plattville again after

school and see how Dwayne's house is coming?" said Georgene. "Just to see if it's worth it."

"I wouldn't risk my life for a house, not even a palace," said Weasel. "If I was Delores, I'd say good-bye to Dwayne. Good-bye to the parachute factory, too."

"What would she do then? Live with her folks forever?" asked Georgene.

"Mom said she could always scrub floors and clean the toilets," Bernie mused.

"Well, maybe I *would* take a chance and jump," said Weasel.

The whole day was spent on parachutes. In art class, each student was supposed to design his own. In history they studied the development of parachutes. In math they studied the velocity of parachutes. Bernie was glad when school was over, and as soon as he had gobbled down some cheese crackers and pop, he got on his bike, rode to Georgene's house, then Weasel's, and together they headed down the highway toward Plattville.

"It's sure been good business for the hotel, hasn't it?" called Georgene over her shoulder, hair streaming out behind her.

"Yeah, I guess so. All the rooms are taken," Bernie yelled back. "People are even paying to roll out their sleeping bags in the lobby."

"I can't believe the parachute factory is making her

jump," said Weasel from behind, where he brought up the rear of the formation. "There's got to be a law against it."

"Why?" asked Bernie. "She's an adult, and they're not forcing her to do it. The reputation of the company is at stake."

"Yeah, but if they're so safety conscious, why did they hire Delores in the first place?" called Georgene. "She can't even make pancakes, much less a parachute."

"Don't ask me, I'm only her brother," said Bernie.

It was a relief to be away from the traffic jam in Middleburg, and they rode single file along the shoulder of the highway, listening to the whir of the wind in the whirligig on Georgene's handlebars, and watching the blur of blue in the crepe paper strung through the spokes of Weasel's wheels.

About twenty minutes later, they came into Plattville, and turned on the side road that led to the excavation site. Once there, they could not seem to stop staring, for springing up out of the deep dark hole that was big enough for a swimming pool or a bowling alley was the steel frame of a large warehouse-looking building that almost resembled an airplane hangar.

"Delores and Dwayne are going to live in a hangar?" asked Weasel. "What are they going to raise? Little airplanes?"

"This is really weird," said Georgene.

Bernie said nothing.

They got off their bikes and walked over to the construction site. The workers were just getting into their pickups, and soon the lot was empty.

Bernie walked around the whole project looking for a sign that said FUTURE HOME OF . . . but he could find nothing that told what it was that was being built, only a small metal sign on a chain around the entrance that said ACE CONSTRUCTION COMPANY, telling who was doing the building.

"I'm going to tell Joseph about this tonight," said Bernie. "Maybe he can call their headquarters and see what they're building."

"Tomorrow's Friday," said Weasel. "That's when Delores jumps."

"I know," said Bernie.

"Well, one thing's for sure, it's not a country home. It's not a mansion. Unless he's got a home somewhere else, he and Delores are going to live in a warehouse, it looks to me," said Georgene.

"I think I should tell her," said Bernie. "I mean, if she's going to jump out of a plane to live in a warehouse, I think she should know."

"Good luck," said Georgene.

They rode thoughtfully back to Middleburg. Weasel thought of all the jokes he'd heard at school that week, and told them to Bernie to cheer him up, but nothing seemed to work.

As they got closer to Middleburg, within five blocks of the hotel, Weasel said, "Do you hear honking?"

"What *is* that racket?" said Georgene. "It sounds like the World's Worst Traffic Jam."

When they got closer still, they could hardly hear each other over the din, for it sounded as though every horn in the town of Middleburg was blowing.

"What *is it?*" Georgene mouthed to Bernie. "What could it possibly be?"

As they turned onto Bessledorf Street, approaching the bus depot, they saw Lester standing out in the middle of the street holding a huge sign on which he had painted:

SAVE DELORES
HONK ONCE IF YOU WANT HER TO JUMP.
HONK TWICE IF YOU WANT HER TO LIVE.

There were so many horns honking that you couldn't tell who was honking once and who twice. Some people undoubtedly wanted her to jump *and* live, so they were honking three times.

Honk! Beep-beep! Toot! Hooonnnk!

Officer Feeney was trying to get through the long

line of cars to reach Lester and pull him out of the intersection. He was frantically blowing his whistle, but it couldn't be heard above the racket.

"Hold my bike!" Bernie said to Weasel, leaping off and scurrying around people's cars. This way, that way, until at last he reached Lester and grabbed the sign out of his hands.

"Do you want to get *killed?*" he cried.

"I'm doing it for a cause, Bernie!" Lester said, his face sober. "I'm trying to save our sister."

"Well, that's noble, but if you get killed in the trying, how is that going to make Mom feel?"

"I don't want Delores to die," Lester said, his lips quivering.

"I don't, either, but standing out here in the street won't help," Bernie told him, and guided him back to the sidewalk.

Gradually the honking died down, and before Feeney could get to Lester to give him a good tongue-lashing, Bernie sprinted the boy away and hid him down in the basement along with Lewis and Clark, who had made the cellar their home for the duration.

"Well, anyway, Bernie, did I stand up to be counted?" Lester asked.

"If I say you did, will you stop trying so hard?" asked Bernie.

Lester nodded.

"Then you did," said Bernie. "That was your moment of courage. Now cool it."

Before dinner that evening, when Delores was in her room trying on her pink jumpsuit, Bernie tried to tell her what it appeared Dwayne was having built over in Plattville, but she waved him off.

"I don't want to know, Bernie. Keep it a surprise," she said. "How do I look? What color socks should I wear, do you think? Pink or white?"

Sixteen

THE NIGHT BEFORE THE BIG DAY

"Will this phone never stop ringing?" Mrs. Magruder said. "Everybody is going to show up at the jump tomorrow morning. It wouldn't surprise me if the president of the United States was there."

"If that's true, my dear, we should fix up the Presidential Suite," said Theodore. "We should order Russian caviar and pheasant under glass. We should have Cherries Jubilee, Bananas Foster, Oysters Rockefeller . . ."

"And a partridge in a pear tree," said Joseph in disgust. "I don't know what's happened to this family, but we just might lose Delores. Did you ever think of that?"

The family grew very quiet, all but Delores, who had decided to take a calming bath and still had not come to the table.

"You don't sound as though you have any confidence in your sister," said Mother.

"Even the most intelligent, trustworthy person can make a mistake," said Joseph. "I certainly wouldn't want to be asked to jump with a parachute *I* had put together."

"Joseph, what you lack is trust," said his father. "If you have no trust in your sister, then trust Providence. If His eye is on the sparrow, then it is surely on Delores, too. For every thing there is a season, a time to rejoice, a time to mourn, a time to spin, a time to weave, a time to work, a time to sleep . . ."

"A time to jump out of an airplane!" said Lester brightly.

"And maybe a time to resign," Joseph added. "I think Delores should resign and find a less dangerous job. I can't believe you're really going to let her jump."

"Look at it this way," Mother told him. "If the parachute opens as we fully expect it to do, her name will be in newspapers all over the country. She will be on the *Oprah Winfrey* show and the seven o'clock news. She will be asked for endorsements and make millions. Men of means will propose to her, and publishers will offer her contracts for her life's story."

"But if she refuses to jump and resigns her job," said Father, "no one will want her. Dwayne Hopper will no longer respect her, neighbors will shun her, and we shall be stuck with Delores for the rest of our natural lives."

"And if she jumps but the parachute doesn't open?" asked Joseph.

"Then it's 'Good night, Delores'!" sang out Lester, but Father thumped him on the head.

"O ye of little faith," said Theodore. "Consider the lilies of the field. Is she not greater than one of them?"

"Now listen to me," said Mother. "I want everyone here to hold hands around the table . . ."

She waited while they all took hands, everyone but Delores, that is, who was still in the tub.

". . . And I want you to close your eyes and visualize your sister jumping out of that plane. I want you to imagine her with her arms outstretched against a clear blue sky, and a white parachute with a blue border billowing out behind her. I want you to imagine her floating down to Earth, gently, gently, and as her feet daintily touch the ground, flashbulbs will pop amid applause and cheers. Reporters will rush to interview her, and bouquets of flowers will be thrust into her arms. Imagine it, see it, hear it, breathe it, and it will happen."

They all sat with their eyes closed, trying to do as Mother requested. Soft footsteps sounded in the hallway, and then Delores's voice cut through the silence. "What's this, a séance?" She stood there in her bathrobe and bare feet, staring at the family.

"My dear, we are sending positive vibrations your way," said her mother. "We want to do everything to make your descent tomorrow a memorable one. Come have some dinner and let us look at our darling daughter who, by this time tomorrow, will be enjoying a victory dinner."

Delores, however, plopped down in her chair without smiling and proceeded to maul a green bean.

"Is something wrong, my dear?" asked her father.

"No," said Delores.

"Is there anything you'd like to tell us?" asked her mother.

Delores shook her head.

"Well, then!" said Theodore brightly. "To Delores, who will make us all proud!" He lifted his water glass and clinked it against the others'.

Georgene and Weasel came over later and sat on the back step with Bernie, eating Mrs. Verona's butterscotch bars.

"Do you think she'll do it?" asked Georgene.

"She doesn't have much choice," said Bernie.

"Do you think the parachute will open?" asked Weasel.

"A one out of ten chance, that's my guess," said Bernie, wondering how he could have been so selfish as to think only of getting his sister's room.

At that moment the door behind them opened, and out came Delores. She was still in her bathrobe and bare feet, and her face seemed as white as milk. She squeezed onto the step beside them.

"Does anyone want to make a quick five hundred dollars?" she asked.

They stared.

"Take my place at the jump tomorrow, and I'll give you every penny in my savings account," she said.

No one answered for a moment. Then Bernie said, "Delores, even if we agreed, they'd never let us do it! You're the only one who can make that jump."

Delores sat with her face in her hands. Then she brightened suddenly and said, "What about dressing Mixed Blessing up in my clothes and sending him up?"

Bernie, Georgene, and Weasel could only stare speechless, and Delores said desperately, "What about all the animals together? Do you think the safety inspector would settle for them instead of me?"

"Are you nuts?" cried Bernie. "Take a chance on our pets? I'd *never* do that to Mixed Blessing. Lewis or Clark, either. And Salt Water would simply fly away."

Delores began to sniffle.

"Delores," said Georgene. "If you're feeling shaky

about this parachute, maybe you shouldn't go up."

"Yeah," said Weasel. "If *I* made a mistake with a parachute, I sure wouldn't risk my neck."

Delores suddenly straightened and asked haughtily, "Who said I made a mistake? It's just the whole spectacle I find so distasteful—the photographers, the reporters"—her lips began to smile—"the attention, the fame . . ." She sighed. "I'm just a simple country girl whom fate has chosen to . . ."

"Ah! There you are, my darling!" came a voice from the darkness, and around the corner of the hotel came Dwayne Hopper. "Delores, my dear, you should be resting. You'll want to look your best tomorrow for the photographers."

"You're absolutely right," said Delores, getting to her feet. "Destiny calls. Good-bye, Bernie. I mean, good night, everybody."

"Sweet dreams, Delores," said Georgene.

Bernie and his friends watched Delores go back into the apartment with Dwayne Hopper, who had his arm around her.

"Bernie, I hate to say this, but she's going to die," said Weasel.

Georgene gave him a poke in the ribs. "Don't be rude."

"I'm not being rude, I'm being honest," Weasel insisted. "If she were my sister, I wouldn't let her go."

121

"You don't even have a sister. You don't know what they're like," Bernie said. "You especially don't have Delores."

"And after eleven o'clock tomorrow morning," said Weasel, "neither will you, maybe."

Bernie got up from the step, went inside, and looked for Joseph. He had to tell him what a strange house Dwayne Hopper was building in Plattville. Somehow, that might be important.

Seventeen

WHAT JOSEPH FOUND

The day dawned bright and sunny.

Bernie started wishing for rain and thunder—anything at all to keep Delores from going up—but he hadn't even got out of bed before he heard the clamor of photographers and reporters from out in the lobby, all wanting to interview Delores, to take pictures of her looking bravely out the window up at the sky, zipping up her pink jumpsuit, and to report what she was eating for breakfast.

By the time Bernie reached the kitchen, they were already pounding on the door of the Magruder apartment, so that Theodore finally decided that a separate table would be set up for her in the lobby where they could photograph her to their hearts' content.

Bouquets of flowers were being delivered by the truckload, and arriving amid the flowers was a wiry little man with gray hair wearing a gray pinstripe suit and carrying a pot of lilies.

"Mr. Fairchild!" cried Mother. "Do come in!"

"Flowers for your beautiful daughter!" said the owner, who was obviously delighted at the crowd waiting outside, the throngs of people who were already gathering in Middleburg Park, and the dozens of photographers who were photographing every inch of his hotel.

"There will be music, will there not?" he asked.

"Yes, Joseph's combo, The Cats' Pajamas, will play a few numbers," said Theodore. "You *did* contact your combo, didn't you, Joseph?"

Joseph and some of his friends played music occasionally for various events around Middleburg.

"Yes," said Joseph, unsmiling. "We're ready to go."

At that moment Delores came down the hall from her bedroom, and Bernie had to admit she looked spectacular. Her blond hair was piled in ringlets on top of her head, her eyebrows were plucked to a delicate line, she wore blue mascara, pink blush, plum lipstick, and had painted a small black beauty mark on her right cheek.

A murmur ran through the crowd as she stepped into the hotel kitchen, and then a great cheer as she

124

walked on out to her special table in the lobby, set with a pink tablecloth and a red rose.

She was photographed from every angle.

Reporters recorded everything she ate: four bites of an English muffin with marmalade, one half of a poached egg, a small dish of strawberries, a bite of banana, two spoonfuls of Grape-Nuts, and a cup of coffee. And hovering intently in the background, attending to her every whim, was Dwayne Hopper, who even answered questions for her when her mouth was full. But the questions kept coming:

"Miss Magruder, how are you feeling this morning?"

"Did your father take out a life insurance policy for you?"

"Do you have a fear of heights?"

"How certain are you that the parachute will open?"

"Do you have any last words for your family?"

"Gentlemen and ladies," said Theodore at last. "My daughter is feeling as wonderful this morning as she looks. She is fearless as far as heights are concerned, she is confident of her parachute, I have not taken out a policy on her life, and I am sure that the last words she will utter before she makes her successful leap will be 'Onward and downward, success only comes to those who dare, never put off until tomorrow what you can do today, and a journey of a thousand miles begins with a single step.'"

The reporters who had been frantically scribbling down each answer began to pause, and Bernie, looking at one reporter's notebook, saw that she had written ETC. ETC. ETC.

The Magruders' pets were clearly upset by all the commotion. Mixed Blessing paced back and forth from window to window in the lobby as though looking for a way to escape. He had already lost his goggles, and he'd stepped on the ends of his flight scarf so often that it hung in tatters around his neck.

Lewis and Clark had gone to the cellar and would not come back up, and Salt Water, wearing his pilot's cap, flapped his wings at the noisy crowd and kept squawking, "Order in the court! Order in the court!" but no one paid him the least attention.

"My dear," Theodore said at last to Delores, "you have a three-hour instruction session before your jump, so I think you should finish your breakfast and do any preparations you care to make."

Delores daintily wiped her mouth on her napkin and, to another flurry of flashbulbs, got up from the pink-covered table with the red rose in the center, blew a kiss to the crowd, and went back into the apartment to brush her teeth.

Mother made all of the Magruders put on their best clothes and pin a red flower to their shirtfronts to show their faith in their sister. Bernie felt sick. He wondered if all the flowers that crowded the lobby would be used to cover her grave, and gave his head a hard shake to get rid of the thought.

A limousine came for Delores, and she and Dwayne grandly got inside.

"It's just as though they are being married!" sighed Mother. "Oh, I wish that happy day would come."

"Good-bye, good-bye!" Delores called to her family. "Mother . . . Dad, I hope you're proud of me," she said. "Bernie, if . . . well, should anything go wrong, as I don't for one minute expect it to do, I want you to have my room. And Lester, there's a five-year supply of Whitman's chocolates in my closet. *Should* anything happen, which it won't, they're yours."

"Wow!" said Lester.

"My darling, you will do just fine," said Dwayne. "Believe me, I would not let you go up if I didn't know you would come down safely to be in my arms again."

Mother dabbed at her eyes.

"Good-bye!" called Theodore. "Keep your chin up, your eyes open, your arms spread, your legs relaxed, your . . ."

"Never mind, dear, I'm sure her instructor will tell her all she needs to know," said Mother.

The limo drove away, and Mother set about planning the reception they would give for Delores after she made her successful jump. Bernie and Lester had to go on to school, though Lester had already confided to his brother that he was playing hooky for the day. Bernie put on his jacket.

"Where's Joseph?" Mother asked irritably. "Is he not even going to be present at this historic jump?"

"He was here earlier this morning," Bernie said. "Maybe he's getting his combo ready to play. I'll see you at the park, Mom. Our class is going to walk over together."

"I understand that the parachute factory has put up folding chairs in Middleburg Park for our family," Father told him. "You may walk over with your class, Bernie, but I want you to sit with us so that Delores can see we are cheering for her when she makes her triumphant descent."

Bernie had never felt so uncomfortable, and not even Georgene and Weasel could cheer him up.

"What's black and white and full of garbage?" asked Weasel.

"I'm not interested," said Bernie.

"Yesterday's newspaper!" Weasel chortled.

"Ho, ho," said Bernie. "I'm not in a laughing mood, Weasel."

At school, too, his class was strangely silent on the subject of Delores's jump. It seemed to Bernie that they looked at him with pitying eyes—the boy whose sister was about to die.

At ten-thirty, Miss Raleigh instructed everyone to put their books away, get their jackets, and line up for the walk to Middleburg Park. When they got there, Georgene and Weasel, as Bernie's two best friends, were given permission to sit with the Magruder family in their time of trial. Bernie quickly found the folding chairs where his family had gathered beside the large roped-off area where Delores was to land when she jumped. Mr. Fairchild, his gray hair combed just so, his mustache turning up at the ends, had arrived in his pinstriped suit and sat beside Theodore. Mixed Blessing, in his cap and goggles, had come, too, and was lying at Mother's feet.

"Popcorn! Get your popcorn! Fresh, salted popcorn!" came the cry, and Bernie turned to see Lester walking through the crowd. "Watch my sister jump with your mouth full of popcorn!" Lester went on bellowing.

"Lester!" gasped Mother.

"Look at that boy!" said Mr. Fairchild. "Why, he's a credit to you, Theodore! He can smell a business opportunity a mile away."

Bernie sat down on a chair beside his mother. Georgene and Weasel sat on the grass. On the other side of the roped-off landing area sat the officials of the Bessledorf Parachute Factory. Everyone seemed to be watching the sky for the first sign of the little plane that would carry Delores over the park.

Minutes went by—fifteen, twenty. The Cats' Pajamas Combo showed up and began tuning their instruments—all, Bernie noticed, but Joseph.

"Where's *Joseph?*" Mother fretted, looking at her watch. "It's ten of eleven, Theodore, and he still hasn't come!"

The combo started to play "Somewhere Over the Rainbow."

At that very moment, Bernie saw his brother push his way through the crowd. His tie was untied, his hair was tousled, his suit coat unbuttoned, and he was panting as though he had run a long way.

"Stop the jump! Stop the jump!" he gasped as he collapsed on one of the folding chairs. "You can't allow it to go on, Dad. I just found out what's being built in the deep dark hole over in Plattville."

"What?" cried Mr. Fairchild.

"The Hopper Textile Products Factory," said Joseph, his shoulders still heaving. "They make shower curtains, sails, tents, tarps, raincoats, canopies, flags, and parachutes."

"*Parachutes!*" cried Theodore.

"Yes. And Dwayne Hopper happens to be vice president in charge of marketing. I think he is behind

130

this whole thing. He wants Delores's parachute to fail so that the Bessledorf Parachute Factory will go out of business and his company can take over."

"Oh no!" cried Mother.

"Stop the jump! Stop the jump!" Father yelled to the reporters.

But at that very moment, The Cats' Pajamas began to play "The Wild Blue Yonder," and from over the horizon came a small blue-and-white plane.

Eighteen

A LEAP OF FAITH

Mrs. Magruder promptly fainted, tumbling right over onto Georgene. If Bernie's friend had not caught her, Mrs. Magruder would quite likely have been lying on the ground.

"The dastardly villain!" Theodore bellowed, shaking his fist at the small dot in the sky, which was growing larger and larger as it approached. It seemed no bigger at first than a gnat, then a fly, then a bee, and finally, it had all the details of a plane.

The cheers of the crowd drowned out Theodore's anguished cries, and all that the Magruders could do was stare at the plane as it droned steadily closer and closer toward Middleburg Park, where the crowd had gathered. A large open space in the middle had been roped off as the spot where Delores would land when she jumped. The plane slowly circled the area, dipping its wings, then headed back up into the sky and circled around once more.

Mrs. Magruder opened her eyes just once, saw the plane dipping its wings, and promptly fainted again.

"Don't wake her," Theodore said grimly. "It's better she doesn't watch. Oh, my darling daughter, what have I let you do?"

"Maybe we could all stand out there and catch her," Lester said, his voice shaky.

"Don't be daft," said his father. "At the rate an object accelerates, a penny dropped from that plane would knock you out. A body dropped from that height would put you six feet under."

Bernie felt he had to do something. "I'll tell the people at the parachute factory! Maybe they can stop the jump!" Bernie told his father, and tore around the roped-off circle to where three officials were standing in their dark gray suits, watching the sky.

Breathlessly, Bernie told his story.

"Stop the jump!" said the first man to the second.

"Stop the jump!" said the second to the third.

"I don't know how," said the third to the second.

"We don't know how," said the second to the first.

"Who has the name of the pilot? What is the

number of the plane?" said the first man to the second.

The second man asked the third.

"I don't know," said the third man, shaking his head. "I think it's back at the office."

Bernie rushed back to his family and told them what happened.

"Where is Dwayne Hopper, vice president in charge of marketing now?" asked Joseph angrily. "Too cowardly to show his face? Hiding off in the bushes?"

"He went up in the plane with her," said Bernie.

Mrs. Magruder opened her eyes at last.

"Delores, Delores!" she wept.

"I shall tear the man apart with my own two hands," said Theodore. "I will break his bones and crack his skull." And then, seeing Officer Feeney walking toward him, he called, "Hiram Ignatius, a murder is about to take place here today."

"What?" cried the policeman.

"Our daughter has been duped into jumping out of that plane with a parachute probably known to be defective," said Theodore. "The culprit is none other than her supposed boyfriend and coworker, Dwayne Hopper . . ."

". . . vice president in charge of marketing at the Hopper Textile Products Factory, a branch of which is being built over in Plattville," said Joseph.

"Maker of shower curtains, sails, tents, tarps, raincoats, canopies, flags, and parachutes," added Bernie.

"His name will live in infamy," Mr. Fairchild put in, tapping his cane on the ground.

Joseph explained how his suspicions had driven him to do some investigating—how he had spent the morning at the library and on the telephone, and had found out just what was being built in Plattville, and why Dwayne Hopper went there on weekends to watch the construction.

"So it isn't a country house for Delores he's building at all!" Mr. Magruder cried. "The man has resorted to cold-blooded murder just to destroy the reputation of the Bessledorf Parachute Factory."

"The cad!" shouted Feeney. "We shall stop this at once!" He pulled out his two-way radio, but the plane was circling back again, and the crowd was yelling so hard that he could not be heard.

This time Bernie could see that a door below the wing had opened. He could just make out Delores's bright pink jumpsuit as she sat on the edge of the doorway.

Theodore rushed to the rope surrounding the empty circle where she was to land, and began shouting, "Delores, don't jump!" but of course Delores could not hear him. Amid the shouting, all the crowd picked up was the word "jump," and so they all began to scream it together:

"Jump! Jump! Jump! Jump! Jump! Jump! Jump!"

Delores appeared to be hesitating, however. There was someone behind her in a blue shirt and pants, the same outfit as Dwayne Hopper was wearing that morning. The person in blue gestured to her, but the figure in pink shook her head.

The plane passed by a second time and had to circle again.

The crowd gave a low moan of disappointment, and Feeney turned his two-way radio on again.

"Stop the jump!" he ordered. "Somebody radio the pilot and tell him to turn that plane around and land. There's a murder about to take place here."

There was a pause, and Bernie held his breath. Then Feeney yelled, "I don't know where that plane took off . . ."

Now the plane was making its third approach.

All the photographers and reporters surged forward.

"I don't think I can stand this," said Bernie, his voice trembling.

"Neither can I," said Georgene.

All Mother could whisper was, "No, no, no!"

Theodore only stared at the sky with a face as set as stone, and Joseph clutched his hair in desperation.

"If only I had investigated the man sooner!" he said. "I suspected him all along! Why did I wait? Why did I wait?"

Now the plane was approaching the park once again, and again the door was open. But this time the pink-suited figure was leaning out the door, one hand on the wing strut, and the figure in the doorway was shaking his finger at her, as though ordering her to jump.

Once again the pink-suited figure shook her head. But then, as the Magruders watched in horror, the man in the blue shirt and pants reached out, gave her a shove, and the body went catapulting head over heels, arms outstretched like a large pink bird, a flip-flop doll, against the blue of the sky and the white of the clouds, tumbling rapidly downward toward Middleburg Park.

Nineteen

LOVE

All Bernie could do was scream. All his family could do was watch. The crowd that had been yelling before for Delores to jump began to sense that something was very, very wrong.

Like a giant making a great sucking sound through a straw, the crowd drew in its breath, and a horrified "Nooooo!" rang through the air.

Mother gave a second shriek and fainted in Theodore's arms.

Joseph covered his face.

Bernie didn't want to watch, but couldn't help himself. It was so awful, he had to see; so terrible, he had to know.

And then the "Nooo!" of the crowd turned to "Ooooh," and the "Ooooh" to "Ahhhh!" for billowing out from the pack on Delores's back was a ball of white that grew larger and larger until finally a great parachute floated above her head, and a great cheer went up from the crowd.

Father was so overcome with joy that he dropped his wife to the ground, and Mrs. Magruder looked up just in time to see her daughter descend royally, gracefully, in her pink jumpsuit below a big white parachute with green and yellow stripes.

Green and yellow stripes?

Bernie, Georgene, and Weasel stared. That wasn't a parachute from the Bessledorf Parachute Factory at all. It must be one made by Hopper Textile Products. Dwayne Hopper must have planned all along for the first parachute not to open, Bernie thought, and made sure of it by playing footsie under the worktable with Delores when the safety inspector came around. He had gotten her so addled and nervous, she would probably have sewn the parachute to her right arm and not even noticed. The fact that the Bessledorf parachute didn't open but the Hopper parachute did was the best way in the world to advertise the reliability of his own product.

"What is the meaning of this?" cried two officials from the Bessledorf Parachute Factory as they came rushing out to where the Magruders stood. "This was all a trick, wasn't it? Where is *our* parachute?"

"*Your* parachute, my good men, did not open!" said Theodore.

"If it did not open, it is because it was improperly made by your daughter," said another official. "And if it was improperly made, she should have refused to jump."

"Forgive her! Forgive her!" Mother begged. "Her brain was so addled by love, she would have done anything for Dwayne Hopper."

" . . . who is no longer employed by our company, beginning now," said the largest of the men, who was probably the president.

Delores's brain was surely addled by something, but whether love or the limelight, one wasn't sure. For she looked as regal as one could imagine in the center of the roped-off area to the huge applause and wild cheering of everyone. Gracefully she got up from the ground, unbuckled the parachute, and posed with one hand on her hip, smiling coyly at the cameras and tossing her blond hair over first her right shoulder, then her left.

"Oh, Delores, my darling daughter!" cried Mother, crawling under the rope and rushing forward to embrace her.

"My princess!" cried Theodore, wiping his eyes as the whole family now rushed to her side.

"I don't really mind not having your room. I guess

I can stand living with Lester another few years," added Bernie.

"Can I still have some of your Whitman's chocolates?" asked Lester.

But Joseph had more serious things on his mind.

"Where is that coward, Dwayne Hopper?" he asked. "Do you know who he is, Delores?" And then, to the crowd of reporters and officials, Joseph said, "He is nothing but an imposter! He maneuvered this whole thing to advertise his own company's parachute. He should be arrested at once."

But neither Delores nor the crowd seemed much interested in what had gone on up in the airplane, for there were more flowers to be delivered, pictures to be taken, autographs to be signed, and hands to be shaken. A squad car rolled up, and two officers got out, escorting Dwayne Hopper over to where Delores was standing in her pink jumpsuit.

Theodore strode up to the man and said, "*You*, sir, are a cad!"

"How so?" asked Dwayne Hopper. "I saved your daughter's life, Mr. Magruder."

"He did, too, Daddy," said Delores. "If it wasn't for the emergency chute he strapped on my back at the last moment, I would be dead by now."

"But we saw him push you! He made you jump!" said her mother.

"Yes, I was scared, and I didn't want to, but now

that I'm alive—and *famous*—I'm glad that I did. Do you think I might make the cover of *People* magazine?"

"Delores, my girl, this man engineered the whole thing!" cried Theodore. "He knew the rule at the Bessledorf Parachute Factory, and was simply using you. He made you think he was in love with you, so discombobulating your brain when the safety inspector made his rounds that you were sure to make a mistake. He never loved you at all."

"On that, sir, you are mistaken," said Dwayne. "True, I observed your daughter in the factory and knew that she had made some mistakes. What better candidate, I thought, to show off the superiority of Hopper Textile Products than your lovely daughter, who looks so beautiful in her pink jumpsuit."

Delores beamed.

"But then, when she wrote me that beautiful love letter . . . ," said Dwayne.

"No, when you wrote *me* a letter. And then the poem," said Delores.

"What poem?" asked Dwayne. "I didn't write any poem."

"And I didn't write any letter," said Delores. They stared at each other for a moment in confusion.

Uh-oh, thought Bernie.

"But I did save your life," Dwayne said.

"He is dishonest, and I want him arrested!"

Theodore bellowed to Officer Feeney, who was holding Dwayne by the arms. "He led my daughter to think that he loved her, when all he was interested in was showing off his company's parachute. He toyed with her affections, tinkered with her emotions, played with her earlobes, and frolicked with her feet, but he never asked for her hand in marriage."

"I do indeed love your daughter, Theodore, letter or no letter, and I would never have let her jump if I'd thought she would not land safely," said Dwayne.

"But you have no grand country home in Plattville, sir!" cried Theodore.

"I never said that I did."

"You don't have a house with a bowling alley, either," said Bernie.

"Or a swimming pool," said Weasel.

"Did I pretend that I did?" asked Dwayne. "I said that what I was building in Plattville was a surprise, and a surprise it is. And now that I have told you the truth, Theodore, there is another matter that must be taken care of."

At that, Dwayne Hopper reached into his pocket, took out a small box, then knelt down on one knee.

"Delores, my beautiful jumpsuit, I mean, girlfriend, will you marry me? I don't live in a mansion, but I have a comfortable home in Plattville, and together, with my business experience and your beauty and fame, we will produce the best parachutes in the whole United States. Please say you love me, too."

Bernie couldn't believe it. Someone was actually proposing to Delores?

Everyone waited—Bernie and his friends, Mr. and Mrs. Magruder, Joseph and Lester, the officials of the parachute factory . . . Bernie began to think about a room of his own after all.

"I am madly, passionately in love," Delores answered, "but I'm sorry, Dwayne, it's not with you."

"What?" cried Mr. and Mrs. Magruder together.

"Then . . . then who?" asked Dwayne Hopper, chagrined.

"The airplane pilot—my parachute instructor—is the nicest, handsomest man I have ever known," Delores said. "I knew it as soon as I met him this morning. All the while you were urging me to jump, Dwayne, he was telling me I didn't have to unless I wanted. And even though I knew you had strapped a second parachute to my back, I decided that any man who would push a woman out of an airplane might also push her out of bed on a cold night. So when I went up in the plane, I was madly in love with you, but when I came down, I was in love with Reginald."

The crowd parted suddenly, and there came a tall blond man with a mustache and biceps as big as baseball bats.

"Reginald!" cried Delores.

"Delores!" cried Reginald.

"Oh, Reginald!" sighed Delores, melting into his arms.

"Oh, Delores!" sighed Reginald, brushing her lips with his blond mustache and gazing into her eyes.

"Oh, puke!" said Lester, turning away.

"My goodness, this has been a day of surprises!" said Mrs. Magruder. "I think we all need to go home and have a nice strong cup of tea."

Theodore turned to Officer Feeney. "Hiram, can't you arrest Dwayne Hopper for *something*?"

"What did he do?" the policeman asked. "He said he loved your daughter. He put a second parachute on her to make sure she reached the ground safely. I can't arrest him for that."

"Nonetheless," said an official of the Bessledorf Parachute Factory, "you no longer have a job with us, Mr. Hopper."

"I didn't think I would," Dwayne replied. "I quite expected to be fired, once the jump was over." He turned to Delores. "But I didn't expect to be turned down and out by the woman I love."

"Sorry," said Delores. "You win some, you lose some, and you have to take the bitter with the sweet. Into every life a little rain must fall, for that's the way the cookie crumbles." And she looked adoringly into the face of the handsome pilot.

145

"Well spoken, Delores. I couldn't have said it better myself," said her father.

Delores turned to the officials from the Bessledorf Parachute Factory. "I suppose I'm fired, too?" she asked.

"Miss Magruder," said the president of the Bessledorf Parachute Factory, "while safety and reliability are our chief concerns, there are no rules where the human heart is concerned. And because your face will undoubtedly appear on the cover of every magazine from Maine to Malibu, we would like it to be the face our customers see when they first enter the door of the parachute factory. Our receptionist is moving to Alaska to study the grizzly, and we would like you to take her place."

"I accept," said Delores and, linking her arm in that of the pilot, she walked blissfully off into the noonday sun.

"All's well that end's well, Theodore," Mr. Fairchild said happily. "There is no hotel in Plattville, and we need not worry about the competition."

Father would keep his job, Bernie realized, and they wouldn't have to rely on Delores to support them.

The crowd began to leave. Lester, who was still playing hooky from school, conveniently disappeared, Mr. and Mrs. Magruder went back to the hotel. Joseph went on to the veterinary college, and Bernie's class lined up to walk back to school.

"I bet you'll get Delores's room after all, Bernie," said Georgene. "I'll bet she marries that pilot."

"I don't know," said Bernie. "She's been in love before. Somehow, men always get away before Delores can get them to the altar. I can't believe she turned Dwayne down."

"Well, here's the problem as I see it," said Georgene. "The men think there's no competition. Until today, she's never had two men in love with her at the same time."

"Yeah," said Weasel. "If you really want her room, here's what you should do: You've got to write her love letters from about three different men, and leave them around where the pilot will see them when he comes to take her out, and . . ."

"Oh, no," said Bernie. "From now on Delores is on her own. If I have to spend the rest of my life on the upper bunk listening to Lester chew potato chips, that's the way it will be."

They stopped talking then, because they'd reached their classroom and the teacher was speaking.

"Wasn't this an exciting morning?" she said. "We are going to study air currents. We are going to study wind and air pressure. I was talking to the pilot who took Miss Magruder up in the plane. He said that if a jumper lands on another's parachute as they descend, it doesn't feel like a cushioned ball of air at all, it's like being on the ground. Your feet feel the wind's resistance in the other chute, and you actually have to 'walk' off the parachute below you and find your own space. Isn't that amazing?"

Everyone nodded.

"In fact," said Bernie's teacher, "I feel that the pilot must have information on a number of different matters, and I've invited him to speak to our class. He was one of the most fascinating people I have ever met . . . ," she went on dreamily. "The strongest, most handsome, understanding, appealing . . ."

"Uh-oh," said Georgene.

"This is where we came in," said Weasel.

"I may be sharing a room with Lester for a long, long time," said Bernie with a sigh.